ART FARM

Marc Dickerson

Black Rose Writing | Texas

©2021 by Marc Dickerson
All rights reserved. No part of this book may be reproduced, stored in a retrieval system or transmitted in any form or by any means without the prior written permission of the publishers, except by a reviewer who may quote brief passages in a review to be printed in a newspaper, magazine or journal.

The author grants the final approval for this literary material.

First printing

This is a work of fiction. Names, characters, businesses, places, events, and incidents are either the products of the author's imagination or used in a fictitious manner. Any resemblance to actual persons, living or dead, or actual events is purely coincidental.

ISBN: 978-1-68433-672-2
PUBLISHED BY BLACK ROSE WRITING
www.blackrosewriting.com

Printed in the United States of America
Suggested Retail Price (SRP) $17.95

Art Farm is printed in Palatino

*As a planet-friendly publisher, Black Rose Writing does its best to eliminate unnecessary waste to reduce paper usage and energy costs, while never compromising the reading experience. As a result, the final word count vs. page count may not meet common expectations.

Edited by Pamela Trudel

"Time is short, my strength is limited, the office is a horror, the apartment is noisy, and if a pleasant, straightforward life is not possible, then one must try to wriggle through by subtle maneuvers."
–Franz Kafka

"You must stay drunk on writing so reality cannot destroy you."
–Ray Bradbury

"Remember to get the weather in your god damned book—weather is very important."
–Ernest Hemingway

ART FARM

THIS BOOK

SHOULD BE READ

LOUD

ONE

It was cold the morning I left. Wind blustering, sky a glacial gray.

Actually.

Let's not begin with the weather. Alliteration was nice, but let's try something else.

The day I got fired I had packed a fantastic lunch. I was really looking forward to it.

No. We'll get to that.

Okay, focus.

Right now, in the beginning, I am walking. *Was* walking.

Correct verb tense is important.

(Note: Maybe drop this intro entirely.)

Don't worry, I am getting better. Really. I just need you to stay with me.

This is all I have.

Right.

Anyway. I was walking.

I was walking across an abandoned parking lot. My legs moved as if on their own, stepping around cavernous potholes, weeds resembling trees sprouting from cracks in the cement. I passed through ghostly visions of cars, specters of desperate, happy consumers scurrying in and out of stores. A former haven of commerce, the dregs of suburbia. My home. I'd be lying if I said I wouldn't miss it.

Then clarity returned, and I remembered the truth.

This is where you've been confined to, done your time. Too much time. Hiding among the commoners, an artist incognito.

Of course, that was all about to change.

It was still dark out. For some reason they wanted me here at an hour I had forgotten existed. That was okay. I reminded myself this was all okay.

Through the morning mist I saw the only other car, a gray Oldsmobile parked on the other side of the lot. The engine was on, smoke billowing from the tailpipe. As I walked toward it I noticed it was parked obediently in one of the faded spots. Remember finding that funny and even letting out a laugh, a blast of hot breath in the icy air.

A sparse, delicate array of flurries began to fall. While I appreciated the aesthetics, I wouldn't normally be outside during such a late-season showing from Mother Nature. Come winter, I hibernate. But I was trying new things at this time in my life. Trying to try new things. That was my whole thing. At the time.

As I approached the Oldsmobile, I remembered that I used to drive the exact same car when I first got my license. Gammy, my grandmother's old junker. That's what I called my grandmother, not the car. She always smelled like cookies. Again, the woman, not the car. The car always smelled like…well, something.

I missed that car, like I missed so many things from my youth. Having recently turned the big 3-0, I found myself overwhelmed by nostalgia. Wanted to immerse myself in its false warmth like a safe, soft blanket.

My legs stopped and I realized I had reached the car. I stood there in the wind and the flurries. Turned for one last glance back at my little car, a million miles away. I had parked in a spot as well.

Exhaling, I turned back toward the Oldsmobile. Opened the door and got in.

The combination of the door slamming and the springy unfamiliarity of the passenger seat triggered something in my brain:

What the fuck are you doing?

Open that door and get out. Get out now.

Old Me was scared, like he always was. Fortunately, New Me wasn't having any of that shit.

I cleared my throat, looked over at a complete stranger.

"Cold out there," I said, rubbing my hands together. The heat was on inside the car, though not to the setting I would have preferred.

The burly man sitting beside me in the driver's seat, with his wool knit cap and puffy coat, didn't even acknowledge that someone had gotten in the car. Just kept staring through the windshield, like he saw something out there no one else could. Other worlds, maybe. He seemed bored.

I decided to elaborate on my initial greeting.

"Freezing," I said.

He stirred now. "Yeah."

"Like the Arctic."

"I noticed."

"I'm just saying, it's really—"

"Can we get on with this? I've got errands to run."

The stranger glanced over at me for the first time. His eyes were sunken, tired. I hadn't expected someone so…indifferent. Didn't he realize how exciting all of this was?

He held out his hand.

I reached into my jacket pocket, unveiled the crisp dollar bill. Unfolded it with a delicate flourish, lowered it into the palm of his hand. His fingers clenched the dollar in a tight fist, and he shoved it into his big coat somewhere. The transaction was complete. There was some grunting as he readjusted in his seat to resume staring out the windshield. I took this as meaning I should talk more.

"So, uh, first of all, thank you for accepting me…um, taking me. Still can't believe this is happening. I guess you're wondering why I'm even here. Well, long story short, I got fired from my job and—"

"Uh huh. Great. Thank you, Mr. X." The man noisily cleared some phlegm from his throat.

"...aren't you curious about why I'm here? How I heard about you?"

"Nah."

"Oh."

"I've met a lot of you people. I get it. You want what they all want."

"Is that so?"

"Yeah."

"Well then. What is it that I want?"

"Easy. You want out."

I thought for a moment. "Well, yes. In a way, I suppose. For a little while at least."

Still not looking at me, the man continued. "Your life's become stagnant. There are too many distractions. You're sick of all the bad news, the constant onslaught of social media, of being 'connected' twenty-four seven. You can't concentrate, get any work done. And you need to get work done, because you've got a lot to say. No one understands or appreciates you as an artist, and you need to be free to create the masterpiece you have inside you. That about right?"

I pulled at the whiskers on my chin. "Okay. But there's more to it than that. Mostly I want to...I don't know. What your card said. Become inspired."

"Great."

"You want to know why?"

The man sighed.

"So I can create my version of the American Novel."

"The Great American novel."

"Hey. You said that, not me."

"You really want this, huh?"

I swallowed. "I need it. More than anything. That's why I'm here."

The man returned to staring out the windshield, the idling motor whirring, rumbling our seats. I joined the man's gaze, tried to see into the cosmos with him. All I saw was blurry whiteness mixing with black. Maybe that was it. Finally he spoke.

"You got a wife?"

"...yeah."

"You tell your wife?"

"Of course. My wife supports me, all the way. Well, wants me to get it out of my system. Says it's a phase!"

He shrugged. "Maybe she's right. I mean, not everyone is the next Stephen King or J.K. Rowling."

"Hey. I'm planning on being a real writer. *Hemingway* ring a bell? Kafka, perhaps?"

"Ever had anything published?" He sounded almost interested.

"I'm currently exploring, uh, self-publishing options."

"I bet. What about an editor?"

"A what now?"

"Right. What's your book about?"

"That's the thing. Not sure yet."

He found no need to stifle an oncoming yawn.

Shaking my head I said, "I just want to create."

The man continued to stare for a moment before suddenly making a move to the gearshift. He put the car in drive, his foot still on the brake.

"All right," he said. "You sound ready. Good luck, Mr. X."

Okay, now I was officially confused.

"Oh. Aren't you going to drive me to…wherever?"

"No. Get out."

"But—"

The man slowly raised his arm, pointed past me to the window. "Get out, and go over there. And get in."

I turned my head and peered through the frosty glass. There was another vehicle that looked exactly like the one I was in, parked only a couple spots over. Strange I hadn't noticed it before.

"Oh, okay," I said.

I'd barely made my exit before the car sputtered to life and screeched away in a haze of pollution.

Shoving my hands in my coat pockets, I began to walk again.

Was all of this meant to test me? To simulate what a true artist must go through? Or was it simply part of the experience? Was I already missing the point by asking questions? Do these drivers secure their own Oldsmobiles or does the organization provide them?

My mind was racing. I was already getting my dollar's worth, as far as I was concerned.

In hindsight, I should have used this extra moment to realize that I should forget the whole thing, get back in my own car, head for the hills.

Instead I opened the passenger door of this other car, got in.

"Cold out there," I said, slamming it.

As before, the man sitting in the driver's seat wasn't looking at me. There was the same air of indifference bordering on disdain. Besides some facial scruff, he even resembled the previous driver, had the same burly frame and sour look on his face. I suddenly thought of *The Wizard of Oz* and the guard at the gates of the Emerald City. *Soft, warm nostalgia. Give me my blanket. Want to go home. Watch TV, movies I've already seen. Suck thumb.*

"You ride in the back," the driver said.

"Oh."

Fumbling to find the handle, I eventually opened the door, did as I was told.

As I settled into the back seat, I hoped this wasn't all a tease, some elaborate hoax. Now that I was so close, the excitement was too much. My blood was pumping, leg shaking. I cried out, "Put the pedal to the metal, my good man!"

His eyes squinted at me from the rearview mirror.

"What?"

"Nothing. Just excited."

The driver eased the car into motion.

I took out my cell phone, began touching the screen.

"No phones." The man actually glanced back over his shoulder this time.

"Oh. Right." I couldn't stop typing.

"Hey…hey. Listen to me. Whassa matter with you, huh?"

"I-I know…"

"You wanna get enlightened or what? Huh?"

"Sorry. Just texting my wife real quick…"

The man reached back and grabbed my phone, tossed it out the window. Discarding my only connection to the world, the last remaining artifact of the Old Me. He flashed a thumbs-up to the rearview mirror.

And we were off.

To my surprise, the driver spoke first.

"You know, I'm writing a book. About a detective with a deep, dark secret: he's a shopaholic. Called *Shop Cop*. People will buy that shit, right?"

TWO

The drive was surprisingly pleasant. At some point I even drifted off in the back seat. One moment I was watching my dreary hometown whizzing by, and the next the driver was passing me a nondescript bottle of liquid and nodding, indicating for me to drink up. It looked like fruit punch. Loving fruit punch, I downed it thankfully.

This was daring, stupid. Something only the New Me would fathom trying.

A dreamless sleep followed. I have no idea how long I was out, only that I woke to a violent rumbling under my seat. Through half-open eyes I gradually realized we were bumping over a narrow dirt trail, immense trees and foliage on either side of us.

Our passage through the forest seemed to last forever. Then towering trees were replaced by clear blue sky, and we were driving across an open prairie. Green and yellow blurs passed by my window. Fields, crops, pens of grazing animals, cows and pigs and sheep. Finally we pulled up to a small old farmhouse.

The house itself didn't exactly match the picturesque surroundings. I attempted to count the horror movie clichés. Broken shutters hung from cracked windows. Jungle-sized bugs skittered over splintered wood, faded paint. The front door creaked noisily with the slight breeze.

Luckily, artists are unconcerned with superficialities such as appearance or size or comfort.

Besides, while the first impression of our living quarters was somewhat lackluster, the land surrounding the farmhouse was seemingly infinite. It would provide ample space for creating, eventually questioning our creations and hating ourselves. Couldn't wait.

I thanked the driver, got out of the car, still a bit woozy from my nap. Stretched, inhaling fresh open air, the overwhelming stench of manure. *Manure.* Yes. I was finally living.

Living on a farm.

This was a farm, apparently.

Weird.

The last time I was on a farm was a field trip in fifth grade when I fed straw to a hungry, slobbering pig and felt oddly aroused. It was one of those inexplicable, painful erections you can only have in your youth. In my defense, it was the most intimate experience I had had up to that point. At that age, tying my shoes gave me a hard-on.

That last paragraph was quite the digression. My apologies in advance for any departures from the core narrative that may occur from here on out. Although I suppose these tangential thought-diarrheas may very well be my best stuff, what I become known for.

> **(Note: You're making it worse. Come on, man. Stick to the story. Describe actions, what happened. You lived it, remember.)**

I signaled for the driver to pop the trunk so I could get my stuff. Remembered I hadn't brought any stuff. Mimed the action of rolling down a window. The driver obliged, shooting me an impatient look.

"Sorry. Don't have any money besides that dollar they told me to bring. But I wanted you to know that I thought about tipping."

He'd driven off before I could scrounge around in my pocket for some loose change.

It was okay. Didn't have any.

Stepping through the doorway of the farmhouse, I was greeted by a décor that one might call "ultra rustic." The only furniture (the only anything, really) consisted of exactly two wooden chairs and a yellowed couch from an indiscernible decade.

There was a jarring, jangly noise and I looked over to discover another person was already there. It seemed he was making himself at home, lying lengthwise on the couch, looking down at a beat-up acoustic guitar he was strumming. It was hard to determine which was the more grungy and worn-out of the three—the man, the guitar, or the couch.

At first glance, he was a man out of time. More specifically, a mid-nineties slacker stereotype that had drifted into the modern age from the nearest 7-11. He had a mess of long greasy hair, was decked out in flannel and faded jeans, a mustache-goatee combo rounding out the ensemble. Could have been a college kid or a burnout in his thirties. And judging from the odor, he fit right in with the other farm smells.

He stopped strumming, shook his head to clear the hair from his eyes.

"Yo."

I pointed. "You have a guitar."

"Brought it." He raised the instrument triumphantly. "Told them I wasn't coming without it. Fuck that. My guitar and I are one. No one's going to push Agony around."

"Cool, man."

"Yeah."

Did he say "Agony"?

Setting the guitar aside, he got up from the couch and wiped his palms on his jeans before extending a hand toward me.

"Agony," he said.

"Tell me about it." I gripped that hand, shook it, as is custom.

"No, I'm Agony. That's my name."

I stared, unsure of how to respond.

"My life is Hell," he said. "Utter pain and despair."

"Ah."

"I'm a poet. Poet-slash-musician. Mostly folk-electronic-dance mixed with spoken word."

"Oh. Cool. Um, Art."

"Right on. Art. That's why we're here. What it's all about."

"Oh. I mean my name…is Art. I'm a writer. Uh, novelist."

"Arthur."

"Art."

"Right on."

"Yeah."

We stood there, staring and nodding.

"But my real name is Art—that's what my parents named me."

"Agony is my real name. It's what *I* named me. Fuck my parents. Especially my dad. Asshole."

"Right."

I smiled, took a step back toward the door.

Run, Art. Just turn around and run.

"You've probably heard of me." Agony stepped forward, jerking his head to the side and staring at me through his hair. "Used to be in a band called SOUND DUNGEON. We rocked pretty hard. Then my bandmates fucked me over. I would hope they all died horrible deaths if I wasn't such a pacifist. That's kinda my thing. Besides being a poet. And a musician. And a chilled-out dude."

"Cool, cool." *If I scream loud enough someone might hear me.*

"So." Agony picked his nose, breathing on me. "Why are you here, Art?"

This perfectly innocent question made me angry, instantly defensive.

"Why are *you* here?"

"I dunno. Wasn't doing much anyway. Besides. It's good to get away from the zeitgeist for a bit."

I nodded. "Yeah. Fuck the zeitgeist."

We continued to stand, nod at each other. Two artists on a noble journey, searching for enlightenment.

"Yo." Agony glanced around. "You able to sneak any weed in?"

THREE

My new friend Agony and I sat cross-legged on the floor, staring into each other's eyes.

Agony suggested the idea, said it would help get the creative juices flowing. He called this act of intense staring "Energy Poems." I wasn't sure what that meant but told him he should trademark it. He told me I was part of the problem. I agreed.

Anyway, we stared.

I tried not to think. Tried to tell my brain to stop fixating on foolish thoughts. Like, the strong likelihood of no one else showing up, the entire retreat being only the two of us. Stuck on a farm with Agony, for who knew how long. On the plus side, "Agony and I" would be a decent title for my book.

We continued to stare. Absorbing the energy around us. Smelling the must and the cow shit. Feeling the drafty air, splinters in our asses. Fuck couches, chairs. We were renegades, creative pioneers, commencing our voyage into the unknown.

A voice in my head said, *Get into it, man.*

"No time like the present."

"Huh?" Agony's expression remained blank. It was clear he was a veteran starer, had much to teach. Or maybe that was just his face.

"Nothing. Just thinking."

"Focus, dude."

"I thought the point was *not* to focus."

"Yeah, but you need discipline. "

"Focus on not focusing."

"Exactly."

"I think I'm starting to get it."

The staring went on for an eternity or maybe only a minute. Either way I concluded that yes, the two of us were the only ones who showed up. I readied myself to scream. Before I could, there was a voice that wasn't Agony's or mine.

"Knock-knock," the person said, not knocking.

Agony and I turned our heads. She stood in the doorway. Female, a woman. New dynamic. She peered out through straight dark bangs with an expression that said, *What the fuck have I just stepped into.*

"Hello," I said in my best Not a Rapist, Murder or Rapist-Murderer voice.

"Yo yo," said Agony.

"Sup," she said, sounding all cool and informal. She looked like an artist, what one envisions one to look like. Pale, skinny, dressed all in black. Stylish. Bohemian. Suddenly I felt very self-conscious. I looked down at my plain department store-bought shirt, my worn pants and shoes.

Do I look...arty enough?

Agony and I stood, took turns clumsily introducing ourselves.

"Art and Agony," she said. "Sounds like a...something. I don't know. I'm not a writer. Ha."

"What are you?" asked Agony.

"What do you do?" I asked at the same time.

"Um. I'm a painter." She was looking at the floor now. "I paint?"

"Right on." Agony was nodding his head. "Is your art, like...modern?"

"Um."

"Postmodern?"

"Post-post? Ha. Whatever. Labels are...whatever. Guess you could call it, abstract?"

"Very cool," I said.

"Nice," said Agony, at the same time.

"Abstract's cool," I reiterated after a brief pause, for maximum awkwardness.

She looked up at us again. "My name is Clorie," she said. "It's a weird name, I know. It's like Lori with a C? I don't get it either. I'm pretty sure my parents were trying to be hip or something. Anyway. I don't care." She cleared her throat, surveyed the room. "So. This is it, huh. Any idea what we're supposed to do now?"

None of us had any idea what we were supposed to do now.

So we chatted, attempted to get acquainted with one another until the others showed up.

"If there are any others," Clorie said, plopping herself down on the moldy old couch. Judging from her face, she had landed on a particularly moist spot.

Agony and I pulled the wooden chairs over to sit in front of her. This, Agony noted, was a perfect formation for Energy Poems. So we started it up again with our newest member, taking turns staring at one another. This time it seemed to work. Actual creative thoughts began to form. I could feel them, banging around the dusty compartments of my brain. Potential ideas.

Okay. Most of these thoughts were about Clorie.

There was something about this strange young woman. She emanated an exciting darkness, a raw and alluring energy. I was instantly drawn in by it, by her.

I stared first at her hair tied tightly in a long librarianesque ponytail, betraying her warm youthful face. Then I made the mistake of looking into her eyes. Found that I was unable to look anywhere else. I was supposed to split up the staring, look over at Agony as well. But my eyes refused to leave her. And when she stared back, I really felt something.

Where did you come from, Clorie? Why are you here?

I felt like such a stereotypical male. Having stereotypical male thoughts.

No, Art. Bad Art. You came here for enlightenment. You came here to create.

Focus. Focus on not focusing.

I stood up, excused myself. My plan was to quickly and efficiently relieve myself, clear my mind. Crass, I know. But it was the only choice I had if I ever hoped to return to a state of pure creativity.

This was when Agony informed me that there was no "bathroom," per se.

"I pissed outside," he said. "I can show you my spot."

"Oh," I said. "That's okay."

Clorie decided to make an announcement.

"I'm not going to fuck you," she said. "Either of you. Or anyone else who shows up. So let's just get that out of the way. I'm here for art, and art only."

"Art?" I said.

"Yes. The act of creating. You can jerk yourselves off all you like, just don't let me catch you blowing on my ear or doing anything weirdly sexual around me. That shit won't fly."

I remained standing, actually feeling the intense urge to urinate now. Guess it had been a long car ride. "Blowing on your ear?"

She shrugged. "My ex used to do it to me. It was creepy, but he did it all the time, so I got used to it. Whatever. Think I might be a lesbian now anyway. Bi, for sure."

I nodded. "Cool."

"Right on," said Agony.

I sat back down, returning to our silent circle of staring.

Unable to focus, my mind drifted.

"How are we going to eat?"

The words were out of my mouth before I realized it.

"Sorry. Meant to think that."

Agony and Clorie stopped looking at each other, turned to look at me.

"Shit." Clorie sank into the couch. "Was hoping I was the only one worried about that. It's pretty obvious though, right?"

"It would seem to be some cause for concern, yes."

"Hmm. Looks like this may be a primitive, back to nature kind of thing." Clorie thought for a moment. "Guess the men ought to make crude tools, do some hunting."

I said, "You're talking about gender roles."

"Whatever. We'll all pitch in. I'll milk a cow. More into that than killing one." She sat up. "Just saying, we're in the middle of nowhere. Can't exactly order take-out."

"And yet we do need sustenance."

"Right, for energy. So we can make art. Also so we don't die. I don't want to die here, if possible. Can't believe there are animals. Can't believe we're on a fucking farm."

I imagined milking a cow. Grabbing a wad of slimy udders and pulling on them until stuff came out. The image of me actually attempting to do this.

Agony looked at Clorie. "Assumed you wouldn't be too worried about food," he said.

Her eyes narrowed. "Why do you say that?"

"I don't know. Figured you, uh…don't eat much."

"Really. Why? A thin woman has to be anorexic, huh?"

Agony shrugged. "I've known some who were."

"Ah, I see. Because all women are the same."

I said, "I don't think this is a good way to start."

Clorie's piercing eyes were on me now.

"Okay. How should we start, Art?"

I stood again. "Let's check out the farm."

The three of us emerged from the shack, gazing around at the endless nothing surrounding us.

I reminded myself to be in the moment, to feel alive.

I shielded my eyes, squinted toward the horizon. There was no sign of the forest or the narrow dirt path that led us here.

A thought I had: *People spend lots of money to vacation in remote areas.*

"Well," I said, "Guess this is it."

"Call me crazy," said Clorie. "But I assumed there would at least be some bare necessities. Heat, running water...I don't know, *food*. Fucking cheese and crackers. Anything."

"Uh." Agony scratched his mousy hair. "There were a couple bottles of wine in the farmhouse when I got here."

"There were?"

"Yeah. I drank them."

I turned to him. "What?"

"I didn't see any empty bottles," said Clorie.

"Smashed them on a rock."

"Ah."

"It was beautiful."

I squinted at him. "Are you drunk right now?"

"Got a buzz going."

"Goddamn it." Clorie stamped her foot in the dirt.

"My bad," said Agony. "I tried to smuggle in weed and percs, but the driver dude tossed them out the window. So we can't get fucked up. But it's cool. We can be, like, high on nature. On life or whatever."

Clorie said, "I think I hate you."

"Hey. It's okay." I shrugged. "Less distractions. Nothing wrong with that."

Clorie looked like she was about to cry. "This is going to be boring as shit."

I looked around.

"I think that's the point."

FOUR

It was nearly dark by the time the others arrived, three in all.

First there was Tomas, a filmmaker.

He spoke loudly with a vague South American accent, in a way that made him sound very enthusiastic about whatever he was talking about. He was also young, in his early twenties, so he hadn't yet had the enthusiasm beaten out of him.

We gave him the one-second grand tour of the farmhouse, our new home away from home. He looked around, taking it all in.

"Nice shithole. Think they have Wi-Fi?"

He had to be joking, but he looked serious.

"Told my followers I'd be posting everyday. There better be fucking Wi-Fi."

Okay, definitely not a joke.

"They let you keep your phone?" I asked.

"No. But I figured they'd have a communal laptop, tablet, something."

It was very possible he was already missing the point of the whole thing.

Still, I decided it was important to bond, artist-to-artist. Asked him what kind of films he made.

"Weird heady stuff. Experimental. Fucks with your mind."

"Experimental."

"Yeah, bro. Scary, too. My movies will fuck you up! Make you shit your pants."

"So, horror."

"I'm an auteur, bro."

"So. Artistic horror."

"Sure."

"…you don't make zombie movies, do you?"

"No, no. 'Infected,' man."

"Oh, no."

Tomas was short but fit, muscular. His chest and arms bulged impressively from his mesh sports jersey or whatever the fuck he was wearing. He had a closely cropped head of thick dark hair and olive skin. I peered down at my pale freckled arms, the swollen gut I called a stomach. Ran my hand over the remnants of what was once a semi-respectable head of hair.

Ah. Inadequacy. Hello, old friend.

"What camera do you use?"

Tomas shrugged. "Whatever. I've shot movies on my phone!"

"Hmm."

"They look amazing, bro."

"Have your films shown anywhere?"

"All over the world, bro."

"So, online."

"Hell yeah."

It was hard to tell if he was playing the part of an ironic hipster or just ignorant.

Either way, I decided he didn't deserve to be with us. Tomas was a *bro*. One who lifts weights, cheers loudly at sporting events, enjoys general popularity. Bros couldn't be artists. That'd mean the bullies who beat the shit out of me in school were living a lie, and that just wouldn't sit right.

The most grievous offense, in my opinion, was his utter lack of cinematic knowledge. He considered anything released before the eighties irrelevant, referred to all older films as "black-and-white movies," and thought Akira Kurosawa was the name of the actor who played Mr. Miyagi in *The Karate Kid*.

"I weep for the future of cinema," I tried not to say.

Tomas looked around. "So. Think they have Wi-Fi?"

Next up we had the obligatory eccentric performance artist.

She sported a ripped jean jacket, short violet hair swept to one side, and introduced herself by reminding us we were all going to die someday. She followed this up by telling us her name. It was Eve-Tron.

"Like a robot?" asked Agony. "Is that, like...part of your performance-thingy? Putting 'Tron' at the end of your name?" It was a fair question.

She only repeated that this was her name, that we had to deal with it. When the rest of us quickly decided we were not going to call her that, she sighed loudly and said just to call her Eve because we were all "fucking sheep" anyway.

Tomas raised an eyebrow. "As in Adam and Eve?"

She shook her head with another dramatic sigh. "Newsflash: the bible is bullshit. Bullshit for sheep. God is made-up. You sheep."

"I thought he was dead," I said.

"You wish."

She was feisty, this Eve. A real wild card.

Eventually we were able to prod her into divulging a tiny bit of her backstory. Found out she came to the retreat mostly because she thought it would be funny. Also she wanted to get out of the city for a bit, away from all the assholes, spend time with some new assholes. Eve did take a liking to Clorie though, even seemed to have a little thing for her. This was made fairly obvious when she sidled up to Clorie, brazenly grabbing her ass and asking, "You into half-Asian girls?" I guess Eve was half-Asian.

As rude and obnoxious as this was, I figured Clorie was still relieved to see another female here. I was relieved as well. Maybe Clorie and Eve would hook up, save me from my inevitable embarrassing infidelity.

Like with Tomas, I made an attempt to connect with Eve one-on-one. Began asking her about the nature of her performance art, prompting a nice warm loogie in my face.

"That's my performance art," she said.

Riveting, thought-provoking stuff.

Rounding out our artistic assemblage was a peculiar older fellow by the name of Leonard Stantz.

The first thing I noticed was his attire. The brown bell-bottomed pants and wrinkled button-up shirt looked like they had been in the closet since the seventies and probably should have stayed there. Wire framed half-moon glasses rested crookedly on his face. He was bald in the center of his dome with wily gray hair coming down at the sides, as if they were trying to escape his head. In a way he looked like an older, crotchetier version of Agony.

Although Leonard wasn't a poet/musician/pacifist. He was a writer.

Yes, he was part of the brethren, cut from the same cloth. So I tried to cut him some slack and not base my opinions solely on his appearance. To be fair, he turned out to be more than a pseudo-intellectual hippie. He was also a hotheaded kook.

"Writer, huh? Me too. Though I doubt you've read any of my books." He squinted at me over his glasses. "I write sci-fi. *Hard* sci-fi. Hardcore stuff."

"Sci-fi, eh?"

"See, why you gotta say it like that? With contempt."

"Huh?"

"Yes, I write about the fantastical. Aliens and spaceships and alternate dimensions. So what." Leonard pointed a bony finger at me. "I bet you're one of those 'literary' guys. Writing for accolades. All style, no story. Make the whole thing about you. Psh. 'Literary.' All it means is you're too good for genre!"

"Well, I haven't exactly written anything yet..."

"You can tackle important sociopolitical issues in sci-fi. It's called a metaphor!"

Leonard came off as eccentric and antisocial. Someone who most likely lived alone with lots of cats. In other words, a writer.

We were interrupted by the sound of Eve trying to dislodge a wad of mucus from her throat. She blew a snot missile out of her nostril before turning to Leonard. "I bet you're into Centaur porn or some shit."

Leonard folded his arms. "It's called lit-erotica."

"Much more tasteful."

"Besides, that's more fantasy than sci-fi. But anyway, yes, I prefer to write in the sci-fi genre. So I like to expand my mind, think outside the box. Go to other worlds! Guess that's too 'weird' for the *general public*!"

"Bro," Tomas said. "Sci-fi is, like, the most mainstream thing ever right now..."

"'Nerd culture,'" Eve agreed. "Shit makes me sick."

At this Leonard nearly fell back out of his boots.

"Ha! I was the original nerd! Grew up on Robert A. Heinlein, Frank Herbert. The hard stuff. These kids today don't even read! They're all too busy watching CGI-saturated superhero movies and dumb Internet videos. No attention spans, no taste." Leonard shook his head at the ground. "I'll be honest...was hoping for at least one other person here closer to my age. But I guess this is it, huh?"

"Hey," I said. "We're all artists."

"Yeah, yeah. I know. Just saying..." Leonard trailed off, still staring at the ground.

Clearly having sympathy for the old man, Clorie smiled and said, "I like sci-fi. Grew up reading it. Was more into fantasy though."

Leonard made a retching sound.

"Not a fan, I'm assuming."

"Nope."

"High Fantasy?"

"Eck!"

"Young Adult?"

"How about Adult Adult!" He was all riled up again.

Tomas nodded. "I feel you, old man. Movies today suck, that's why the world needs filmmakers like me. Someone who takes risks. Those authors you mentioned sounded cool. I would look them up, but they took our phones. And there's no Wi-Fi. Apparently."

A wild grin spread across Leonard's wrinkled face.

"Good! Less radiation waves goin' through our bodies. And don't worry, you'll survive without telling everyone in the world what you're thinking every second of the day. If your generation can even fathom such a thing."

"For a science fiction author, you're not very 'pro-technology,'" I noted.

"Ha! That's exactly why I'm against it! I've read the stories, thought through all the scenarios. Advanced technology will destroy us all! Wipe out the entire human race."

"Good," said Eve. "Wish it would fucking hurry up."

FIVE

No one else showed. This was it, the six of us. An artistic assemblage of the ones who dared abandon their homes, their lives, go where few if any artists had before. A farm.

Yes. It was really sinking in now. The fact that we had no idea where we were or how long we were going to be here—no clue at all really of what was going on.

But before we had a chance to discuss how blatantly insane all of this was, we realized we had other concerns. The last remaining glow of the setting sun, our only light source, was now fading from the windows. We supposed this meant it was time to call it a night, get a fresh start in the morning. Though there were no beds or pillows or blankets, we tried our best to settle in and get some rest.

I saw Clorie lying on her back on the floor, walked over to her.

"How you holding up?"

"I'm pissed. Can't believe that bastard 'called' the couch." Clorie lifted her head to shoot an annoyed look over at Agony, who was somehow already passed out. Her head thudded back to the floor. "Ow. So this is it, huh?"

"Seems like it."

"Ugh."

"Maybe food and blankets arrive tomorrow?"

"What have we gotten ourselves into. They expect us to live like this?"

I glanced around. "Well. The UNABOMBER did it."

"That's not exactly comforting."

The living arrangements weren't ideal, but I chose to imagine it like we were a bunch of new friends at summer camp.

Except, of course, for the lack of food, running water, electricity, emergency services, or adult supervision. At least we still had the bug bites.

I wondered aloud if we should all cram together for body heat. Clorie suggested we make a fire instead. I replied that was a good idea and hoped someone knew how to do that.

Soon we were all outside under the stars (which I'd forgotten existed), huddled around a roaring fire. Leonard volunteered to start it, and now he stoked the embers, proudly regaling us of his years as a boy scout back in the 1800s or whatever.

Despite Leonard's rambling and the lack of marshmallows or wieners, the warmth of the campfire was pleasant. A chorus of crickets joined the cracks and pops of the fire, and soon the pseudo summer camp spirit really did catch on.

A suggestion for a group exercise was brought up. We would go around the circle, naming major artistic goals, what we hoped to achieve.

Of course, Agony's plan was to conquer the slam poetry world. Also to tour as a solo artist, really stick it to those bastards still masquerading as SOUND DUNGEON. Beyond that, he wanted to focus on keeping his blog page up to date.

Eve didn't care about plans, had no regard for legacy. The concept of immortality through one's work amused her. As she put it: "We'll be dead anyway so what will we care?" This was certainly one way to look at it.

Our self-proclaimed cinephile Tomas told us about the epic horror-art film he wanted to make, called *The Gator People*. The basic plot stemmed from an alligator being inseminated by a murderous psychopathic vagrant. This, in turn, results in the monstrous offspring emerging from the swamp, wreaking havoc on the nearby city. I wasn't quite sure where the "art" aspect came into play, unless the entire film was ironic or a metaphor for something, which I was almost positive it wasn't. Clorie opposed the exploitative nature of the whole idea, said she thought violence was a cheap crutch in storytelling. I nodded emphatically, as to not let on that I thought violence in movies was sometimes cool.

Clorie planned on designing a massive art installation—specifically, a giant flaccid penis—to be placed outside a prominent politician's headquarters in downtown New York City. Now, I don't want to name this politician, as it may date the novel you are now reading. Feel free to substitute your own current vile, abhorrent, repulsive figurehead instead.

Leonard described his vision for a science fiction opus, an ambitiously massive saga. It would encompass at least twelve volumes, each volume consisting of multiple books. Hopefully he planned on beginning soon. Didn't see him getting past the third book before keeling over from alcoholism or heart attack. He was a writer, after all.

"It's gonna be the most epic epic of all time!" The flames in his eyes only enhanced the craziness.

"Hey, let's scream shit out." Tomas was wide-eyed as well, nodding emphatically. "Whatever's in our head at the moment."

"Tomas sucks monkey clit!"

Eve really never missed a beat.

Tomas shot her a look before countering with, "Eve is a deranged dirty bitch!"

"Tomas is a smelly arse tit!"

"Eve…is…she—she really sucks!"

"This is healthy!" added Agony.

Eve pushed herself back onto the grass. "Why the hell did I come here!" She closed her eyes, shouting up at the stars. "Get me away from these stupid smelly losers!" She broke into wild laughter, writhing around, smacking her palms on the ground.

Now that everyone's focus had drifted to this new exercise (attention spans aren't long among artists), it seemed I was in the clear as far as proclaiming my own creative plans.

I was breathing a sigh of relief when Clorie interrupted the shouting. "Wait, we didn't finish learning everyone's goals…" She smiled, turning. "Art?"

My breath caught in my throat.

Dreams, goals.

Just say something, Art.

"I want to write a novel."

The words hung there in the cool night air. Glowing faces stared back at me in the crackle of the campfire.

Leonard scratched his head. "Well, yeah," he said.

"But what do you want to, like, *do*, man?" Agony asked this in his Really Deep voice.

Perhaps I wasn't being clear enough.

"I want to be a novelist."

"Right on, right on…okay. But what's, like, a *feeling* you want to evoke. Or something."

"Feeling?"

"Yeah." Agony was nodding. "Like, how you want the reader to feel."

"Well." I tapped my lips. "I want them to feel…good? I guess?"

"Oh, Gord." Eve slapped her hand to her face.

Leonard looked over at her. "Who's Gord?"

"I made him up. Instead of saying one made-up person's name, I say another."

Gord was a dumb name, made me think of someone I hated.

Looking around, I saw that everyone was still expecting more of an explanation from me. So I used my creative writer mind to quickly come up with some bullshit to say.

"The written word is the purest art form."

The group considered this for a moment.

Tomas shook his head. "Nah. Cinema is truth, dawg."

"What about painting?" Clorie said.

"Or poetry," added Agony.

"Performance, fuckers." Eve punctuated this with a gnarly gob of spit into the grass.

As they stared back at me a noncommittal shrug was all I could offer in response. "Eh...I don't know...maybe." My gaze drifted to the crackling fire, and we all sat together in silence for the first time since we had arrived on the farm.

The excitement of our first evening was winding down. I wondered how much my lackluster response had to do with that. Everyone seemed bummed out and tired now.

We attempted sleep again, shadows of flames flickering and dancing over our shivering bodies.

Hands behind my head, I gazed up at the brightly speckled sky above. Stars, man. Never even thought about them before, and yet there they were. All that faint, fading light amid all that blackness. Dotting the mysterious void, the infinite expanse of planets and galaxies, other worlds we'll never see or know.

The moon. People walked on that once. Pretty crazy, when you think about it.

Something was stirring in me, yearning to get out.

My head buzzed. Was this inspiration?

Mostly what I felt was discomfort due to the chill in the air, the pebbles under my ass. Oh, and hunger. I definitely felt hunger. The realization hit me that I hadn't eaten since that morning's quick stop at McYumYum's on the way to the abandoned parking lot, what felt like a thousand years ago already. None of us had. Except Agony, who'd somehow snuck in a candy bar. I didn't want to know where he had stashed it this whole time. He was unwrapping it now.

I watched him take a bite, a long strand of nougat dangling from his mouth as he stared into the fading light of the fire. His eyes were big, like a child's.

"I don't know, man," he whispered, chewing. "How long until we slaughter that cow?"

SIX

Warm sunlight stirred us awake. My fellow artists and I sat up on the grassy earth we now called our bed, looking around at what was now our home. Our sleep may have been restless, but waking to this strange new world provided its own form of rejuvenation.

The time had come to work. To create. It was either that or have the saddest, weirdest orgy imaginable.

Leonard clapped his hands together. "All right! Rub those crusty peepers! We've got a full day of *creating* ahead of us. What could be better?"

"My phone?" Tomas stood, stretched. "And a charger for my phone."

Leonard shook his head, chuckling to himself. Then something offensive seemed to hit him, causing him to hold his nose and wince in exaggerated revulsion. "Wooieee! Man. It stinks!"

The rest of us looked at him, confused.

He waved his hand around in the air. "Damn. What did they do, build this place next to an old toilet factory?"

"Um. We're on a farm," I pointed out.

"Animal shit..." added Clorie.

Leonard chewed his lip. "Yeah. I've been pondering that...why a farm? Why aren't we, say, at a lake? A mountain? Hell, why not a tropical island?"

The group responded in tired shrugs and mumbles.

"Animals are cool." Agony swatted at a fly. "Better than the bugs."

"Still don't understand if we're supposed to be taking care of the animals." Clorie was watching a herd of cows in the distance. "Should we, I don't know, milk them?"

Agony joined her gaze. "Shit, you're right. Don't want their udders to explode."

"Wait." She looked at him. "Does that...happen?"

"That's not our concern." Leonard was squinting off toward the horizon now. "I'm sure they have workers who take care of all that. I mean, the land appears to be maintained. There's got to be someone here other than us."

"Yeah, I guess so..."

"We're here to create, remember? Heh. Actually! Who cares why we're on a farm. It doesn't matter!" He looked around at us. "No matter where we are, we need to rely on our minds, our instincts. Get primal. Like our ancestors. Paint on walls. Smear dirt on our bodies."

Clorie's attention was still on the herd. "If cow udders start exploding I'm going to be very upset."

Tomas nodded at Leonard. "Yeah, man. I'm ready. Think I'm starting to get it. Get why we're here."

Clorie turned back toward the group. "That's impossible. You can't be *getting it* already."

"Psh. You're just mad 'cause you're not getting it."

"That's stupid. You're stupid."

"I gotta piss," I said.

"Where's Eve?" someone asked.

Right on cue, Eve's partially shaven head emerged from behind a grassy slope.

"Morning fuckheads," she said. "Come check it out."

We followed Eve down the other side of the hill to where her discovery loomed before us.

At first glance the lone shack appeared to be floating. An eerie mist billowed around it, making it look like it was in the middle of a vortex, some mysterious nether region beckoning us to go inside.

"Let's go inside," I said.

Stepping through the doorway and onto the floorboards, we stood there in shock. There were *things*. Things everywhere, cluttering the space. Artistic things, it seemed. Things to help us create.

We gazed open-mouthed from one corner to the next, taking in the various resources at our apparent disposal. Everything from painting and writing materials to musical instruments to desks and chairs. There was filmmaking equipment too, vintage and newer cameras side by side.

"TV," Tomas said, pointing.

Everyone's head turned at the same time. There it was, mounted on the wall. A shiny new widescreen TV.

A moment of astonished silence followed before Clorie uttered, "Wait, so we do have power?"

Leonard raised his eyebrows. "Well. That TV is plugged into *something*."

Like kindergarten kids racing to claim the best blocks at playtime, we made a mad dash over to our new toys, heading straight for the entertainment center. We stared up at the glorious monument called television, its blank screen already mesmerizing, calling out to us. The void pulsed with endless possibilities of pure happiness. *Oh wise one, entertain us. Aid us in our time of need.*

"It *is* plugged into something..." Leonard was inspecting behind the entertainment center before looking back at us. "There must be a generator on this farm."

"Well fuck." Tomas pushed his way to the front of the group. "Turn it on. Maybe they got HBO." He licked his lips, looking around at us excitedly. "This probably means there's a router somewhere too. We're 'bout to be plugged in, baby."

Eve was the only one who hadn't joined our foray back into the sweet comforting arms of consumerism. She was still near the doorway, arms crossed, observing us with utter disdain (even more than usual). A sudden wave of shame came over me. One glimpse at a TV and we were ready to give in once again to the convenience of modern technology, to bow at the feet of the nostalgia gods.

"I knew it." We all turned to face Eve's disappointed glare. "You're here for one day—not even one day—on what is supposed to be a *retreat* from all of this shit. And the first thing you want to do is turn on a TV. Ugh. Fucking sheep."

"*Bah*, baby." Tomas flashed a smile.

"Ew."

I glanced around at the others. "I was just wondering if it worked. You know. For curiosity's sake."

"Same." Clorie nodded, clearing her throat. Her eyes darted back to the TV. "Although…they must have given it to us for a reason."

"Yeah, they did." Tomas still had a big smile on his face. "To watch the badass movies I'm about to make!"

Eve rolled her eyes. "*Bad* being the operative word."

Agony waved his hands in the air. "Yo yo, guys. Listen. Eve is right. All this materialistic shit. We don't need it. You know?" He gestured to the TV. "Let's, like…*not* turn it on."

"I already turned it on."

We looked over at Tomas with the remote in his hand, then up at the glowing screen.

I will not lie. It was a beautiful moment.

However, the joy did not last long.

"'A/V Input.' The fuck does that mean?"

"Press another button," I urged, a slight sweat breaking on my forehead.

"I…I am." Tomas was pressing every button, moving toward the TV. He squinted up at the screen, intensely focused, willing something to appear.

Clorie had a thought. "Maybe…we're supposed to make our *own* stuff. To watch on the TV."

"Yeah." Eve grinned over at Tomas. "Listen to the smart lady. Make a film, fucko."

Tomas put his hands on his hips, glaring at Eve defiantly. "I will! One that will blow your mind, chica."

"Did anyone ever tell you how dumb you are?"

"Only how dumb I'm not." Tomas grinned again. Eve rolled her eyes.

Leonard sidled up to Tomas. "You going with film or digital?"

"Definitely film, bro. Old school."

"Right on. Gotta keep it alive."

I felt the need to interject.

"You do realize film is a lot more…complicated. Right?"

"Went to film school, bro. Spent some time with lovely lady celluloid. I got this."

Tomas was confident, at least. Which was more than I had.

When the hell was the last time I even wrote anything?

A thought crossed my mind, a voice rudely screaming that I was a wannabe, a fraud.

What are you even doing here, Art?

I missed my wife, my dog. Never mentioned my dog. Farley. Little guy was probably bummed my unemployed ass wasn't home dropping him crumbs all day.

Leonard moved to the front of the group and straightened up with his chest puffed out, looking like he was about to address an army of Vikings.

"All right, everyone. I propose that each of us spend the first day brainstorming, working on our respective projects. This evening we'll gather 'round the fire to discuss, get some feedback."

The group muttered in agreement, except for Eve.

"Nah, I'm good," she said. "I don't care what anyone thinks. Especially you assholes."

Of course.

Still, Leonard's idea was some sort of plan, a course of action. And even though we were free to create as we pleased, a bit of structure wouldn't be the worst thing. At the very least, it might help us forget the extreme hunger pangs.

"Hey, what about food?"

Shit, thanks Agony.

"Right." Leonard nodded. "Well, I don't mind spending my first day on the farm foraging. Performing menial tasks usually helps me focus on book ideas anyway. I'll try and find some berries, water.

There's got to be a stream or lake close by. I mean, we're on a fucking farm. Must be *something* growing around here."

None of the crops I had seen looked ripe enough to eat, but far be it from me to let any steam out of Leonard's proud moment of martyrdom. In fact, I decided I would try and put some oomph into the proceedings, get everyone into the spirit.

"Okay, team…" I said, reaching my hand into an imagined huddle. I wasn't sure what I was even doing, only that I had seen athletes do this in sports movies before a big game.

My hand hovered there, waiting for other hands to pile on top of it in some form of gregarious gesture.

This did not happen.

Instead everyone stood there, staring at me.

Eve broke the silence, jerking a thumb in my direction.

"Who invited this guy?"

SEVEN

The work began.

Our first official day was spent utilizing our newly discovered shack and the creative tools inside. Except for Leonard, who was off in his attempt at foraging. I figured he'd already gotten sidetracked, was now hunting for crop circles.

Tomas was determined to make something straight away with all the film equipment, mostly to spite Eve I assumed. After trying and instantly failing to get the older film camera to do what he wanted it to, he grabbed the digital camera and asked Eve to be his star. Eve—being Eve—laughed in his face. At least there was no saliva involved.

However, eventually she gave in and they went off to shoot a movie. It was cute really, the two of them helping each other out, all for the sake of art.

That left Clorie, Agony and I in our cozy little work studio. We weren't quite as sure how to begin. For a while there was a lot of pacing and tapping of chins. Clorie eventually got busy splattering paint onto a canvas. Agony continued to pace, but now with notebook in hand, pen in mouth, muttering to himself.

I sat with my feet propped up on a small wooden desk, gazing out a spiderweb-infested window. On the desk was a pad of paper with a pen resting on top of it.

This was it. The moment I had been waiting for.

Nothing to do now except…write.

Okay. Let's do this.
Writing. Creating.
Yes.
Here I go.
About to write. Write some words.

I watched my breath in the air, felt a shiver. *Still no heating system, I guess.*

The electrical power on the farm seemed strictly limited to creative pursuits. Beyond that there wasn't much in the way of convenience. And we still didn't have cell phones, the most convenient modern convenience of all.

I shook my head, tried to focus.

Bukowski. Hemingway. Steinbeck. All those dead fuckers. I called upon their energy. Beckoned the spirits of the great authors to flow through the fields, through the window of that shack and into my body. Hoping to receive even an ounce of whatever it was that allowed them to create such formidable output.

Take Bukowski. Through his work I discovered a prose that was oddly eloquent while still retaining a stark ruggedness. His stories didn't involve intricate plots and he never wrote any sweeping epics, but Charles Bukowski attacked the craft with ferocity, something you felt. His writing was uninhibited. There was an undeniable energy, a personality.

Granted, much like his characters, the man was a drunk, a scoundrel, a womanizer. Some would argue he was nothing more than a crude lowlife with a gambling habit and a typewriter. And maybe they're right. But must all creators be perfect, shining examples of human beings? I'd argue it's the flaws and the imperfections that helped create the work, as much as anything else.

The man could write. That was all that mattered.

I wondered what it felt like. To be able to write like that.

Hemingway—clearly an influence on Bukowski, as well as countless others—once said, "All you have to do is write one true sentence. Write the truest sentence that you know."

Okay.

Sure, easy for him to say. Finding the truth isn't so daunting when you're on a liquid diet of boilermakers and imported red wine.

Why did Agony have to drink all the damn wine?

I know. I shouldn't need to be intoxicated to write. The farm itself should be all the inspiration I need.

Maybe that's it. Write about the farm. Yeah. The animals. Make them into something, an allegory. Anthropomorphic caricatures from different sociopolitical backgrounds!

Oh, wait…

Fuckin' George Orwell.

I switched gears.

Write what you know. That's a good way to start.

Maybe write about my childhood.

Fuck. That won't work. I didn't do anything.

Mostly read books.

Nobody wants to read about you reading, Art.

Okay. Fair enough. What else? Parents argued a lot, threw things at each other. That's good, right? People read about stuff like that.

"People, man," I heard Agony say. He was still pacing and muttering to himself. "They just…don't get it."

He stopped to jot something down in his notepad, tongue hanging out not unlike a dog. It must be important to document ideas quickly before they evaporated from one's burned out, weed-infested brain. I watched him click his pen, nodding to himself in satisfaction.

My gaze drifted over to Clorie. Her painting had only just begun and already it looked incredible.

She paused, dabbing the palette with her brush. "You think Leonard will find anything?"

I looked down at my notepad and then up again, pretending to come out of deep concentration. "Huh? Oh. Yeah. As long as he doesn't get lost. Or abducted by aliens. Seems like the type that would happen to. I'm sure he'd be thrilled."

"Come on. He's not that bad. Just…peculiar."

"That's one way of putting it."

She shrugged. "Seems to have a grasp on what he's doing. Well. More than us."

"Let's hope so."

A shriek of distortion interrupted our conversation. Agony had gone electric. Must have found a guitar amp.

Clorie turned and tried her best to smile in the direction of the noise, her eyelids fluttering to each jarring note. "Very nice," she managed.

Agony stopped strumming. "Thanks." He stared blankly before saying, "...like, I got this one song I just came up with."

"Oh. Cool."

"...wanna hear it?"

Clorie nodded, the instant regret of what she had gotten herself into showing on her face.

"Of course, sure..."

Agony strummed again, his voice straining in some mangled form of melody.

> *I just keep fallin'*
> *Fallin' down the hill,*
> *I just keep fallin'*
> *And I know that I will...*

When the last murky chord finally rang out, Clorie clapped politely, straining her face into another smile. "Great song! It's kind of like...a metaphor."

Agony stared back with his usual vacant expression.

"What?"

"Huh?"

"What is?"

"Hmm?"

"The meta...wait, what do you mean?"

"You know." Clorie shrugged. "About life. Going up that hill. You're saying, some of us keep falling. Right? But all we can do is pick ourselves up and try again."

"…oh."

"Oh. Okay. Hmm. You mean, that's not what you—"

"It's based on an actual event."

"Ah."

"From my life."

"You mean you were—"

"Falling."

"Like, literally."

"Yeah. Down a hill."

"Right. Okay."

"It sucked."

I zoned out at this point. Had a hunch once you dove down the well of Agony's stupidity you'd be going on a long, dark journey.

And yes, that would be a metaphorical well.

After another hour or so of sitting there, I decided I should get down to business.

Wait, I haven't even figured out what kind of story I want to write.

Slice of life character study? Dickensian epic? Sleazy dimestore trash?

Shit. Do people even read books anymore?

Somewhere off in the distance, a cow mooed.

Did that mean something?

I looked down at the desk.

Oddly, the desk stirred something in me.

Suddenly I was transported back in time. I was at a different desk, one cluttered with paper and an outdated computer. Walls appeared, closing in around me. Yes, I was back at my mind-numbing office job, in my tiny cubicle, basting, wasting away. Closing my eyes, trying to float away, into a world of my own.

The opening scene appeared before me:

An office floor bathed in oppressive fluorescent light, filled with identical-looking human drones performing repetitive tasks, zombie-like. Inane chatter from irritating cubemates, fingers clacking away on keyboards, printers loudly printing. And in the midst of it all: me. Another cog in the wheel, carrying out the evil hierarchy of nepotism and greed, all for the sake of a steady paycheck and a dental plan.

I shuddered.

My thoughts flashed back to one scene in particular: my last day.

Hey, flashback. There's a novel idea.

USE OF A LITERARY DEVICE
I

As usual, I was thinking about lunch.

Lunchtime. The one bright spot of the day, something to look forward to.

There was nothing fancy about the contents of that wrinkly brown paper bag. Still, it was better than thinking about my job.

My department at Berger & Balki & Associates wasn't exactly a cheerful one. On the Foreclosures Team, it was our job to ensure that corporations succeeded in getting richer, while making sure families already on hard times lost everything they ever earned. So my main daily task was to put the reality of what I was actually a part of out of my mind.

On this day (as on many others), I sat in my cube in front of my computer, attempting to break my previous record for chair-leaning. I had gotten pretty good at my balancing act, gambling with gravity just to the point of falling backwards on my ass in a total wipeout. It was exhilarating.

The corporate world, man, I remember thinking, staring up at the air vent, stale heat blowing my face. *That Dilbert knew what he was talking about.*

After graduating college with my much sought-after General Communications degree, I banged around in a multitude of menial desk jobs, all of them equally banal. But Berger & Balki introduced me to a whole new level of soul-killing. Hell, I'd only been with the company for a year and I was already a walking corpse.

Recently turned thirty, which didn't help. Already sensed my body giving up on me, shrugging as if to say, Well, *we had a good run*.

My mind wasn't doing much better.

Some thoughts likely floating through my brain:

Time is going to crush me.

Time doesn't even exist. But it's all I think about.

You waste all your time, working your life away for a company that doesn't care about you. You work and work and then one day some overworked employee comes in with an AK-47 and shoots up the place and that's it.

I should be making the most of my time. Instead I spend it here, working.

We're all just dying animals screaming for someone to look at them.

You know. Normal, well-adjusted thoughts.

Lunchtime, though. That would be glorious.

What did this lunch consist of, you surely must be wondering?

The main attraction was the thinly sliced turkey and American cheese on wheat bread. Little bit of mayo. Simple, classic.

The sandwich was accompanied by grapes (purple) and chips (ridged, plain). And finally, the last piece of Bundt cake, leftover in the fridge for a debatable amount of time, but nonetheless an exciting way to top off the meal.

Man. I was really fucking hungry.

I tried to focus on my job, really. Tried to find something fulfilling about it. Nothing came to mind. Not even my latest score of stolen office supplies (glossy computer paper, a box of shiny new paper clips) or sipping cup after cup of shitty office coffee provided me any gratification.

Still, something in the back of my head told me I had to keep going, keep fighting the good fight in what remained of my short, feeble time on this planet.

I'm special. I'm somebody. I know I am.

I had to be. Otherwise, nothing meant anything.

As I sat there, contemplating the bad workplace sitcom my life had become, the usual cacophony of office jargon crept in around me:

"Appraisals."

"Writs."

"Liens."

"Lenders."

"Deeds."

Of course, this was sprinkled with the requisite athletics blather:
"Game."
"Team."
"Win."
"Lose."
"Suck."

Swiveling my chair to face the window, I looked out over the grimy, dirty, magnificent city, glittering, bathed in golden light. The sun peeked out around concrete and metal, shining down on the bustling denizens below.

A tiny bird was hopping along the window ledge, as if it were so easy to be free.

Turning away from the bird and the temptation of the outside world, I stared down at my desk, imagined doing myself harm. Specifically, I fantasized about placing my hand beneath the large stapler and pounding down on it with my fist. Hard.

Such violent visions had become alarmingly routine, provided a fleeting moment of exhilaration.

I'm going to do it this time. No one can stop me.

Heart racing, I leaned forward, globs of perspiration splashing onto my keyboard. Felt the sickness swelling within me. Realized I wasn't reaching for the stapler, I was reaching for a pen. Held it in my trembling hand, above an open notepad. The pad meant for notes from client phone calls was suddenly the most beautiful thing in the world to me: a blank page.

Tongue flicking in and out of my mouth like a deranged lizard, my hand steadied, and I brought the pen down until the tip touched paper.

"Hey! Art the Fart!"

My hand jumped, pen ripping through the paper like in a cartoon. Noticed my co-worker, Gord—resident goober—standing on the other side of my cubicle, casually resting his morning mug of coffee on the divider.

Gord was around my age, hairline on the same receding schedule as mine. What was left was over-gelled and combed upwards, as if the height would distract from the lack of volume. Everything about him was obnoxious.

I turned to look up at his dumb face and his dumb hair. He always had this big toothy grin on his face that gave me nightmares. His general aura was one of stale coffee breath and intense cologne.

Wasn't crazy about his personality either—rather, the lack thereof. See, Gord was an empty vessel. A company stooge, the kind of person that seemed to exist only within a corporate environment, no thoughts in his head beyond the next coffee break.

Sure, I looked forward to my lunch. But I had dreams, damn it, plans for the long-term. Even if I wasn't sure what they were yet. Gord's only aspiration was happy hour at the bar next door, continuing his nightly tradition of drinking himself into oblivion and aggressively hitting on co-workers. Though I suppose one needed respite after a long day of spreading gossip and annoying others.

"Watch that game last night?" He grinned his unsettling grin before adding with a snicker, "Oh, I forgot, you don't watch sports."

"I do watch sports…sometimes," I heard myself point out meekly. What was I even defending? I don't give a shit about sports. The most excited I get over anything remotely athletic is when shuffleboard makes its appearance at the Winter Olympics.

Gord slurped his coffee, eyeing my desk. "What you got there? A book?"

I looked over at the most recent novel to occupy my workspace.

"Yeah. It's a book."

"That's dumb. Why do you always have books with you? What do you, like, read?"

"Yeah. I read."

"Like on your breaks and stuff?"

"Yeah."

"You're fuckin' weird, Art. Who reads anymore?"

"I mean, plenty of people—"

"Damn, you're boring, Art." Gord stretched with a big animated yawn. "Hope you don't mind, but I'm looking forward to getting a new neighbor soon. Word around the office is there's going to be some seat shuffling." He wiggled his eyebrows comically. "That new redhead in accounting wouldn't be too bad. Oh, man. Daddy like."

"Uh. Haven't seen her." I turned to my computer screen, shuffling papers, pretending to get back to work.

"Tits are fuckin' huge. Big ass, too."

"Yeah?"

"Mmhmm."
"Big, you say?"
"Oh yeah. Big ol' butt."
"Nice."
"Yeah, I'd like to..."
BEEP.

That was the intercom buzzing through the speakers.

"WOULD JASON BUTLER IN ACCOUNTING PLEASE CALL EXTENSION 9142, THANK YOU."

These announcements never remotely pertained to my job. I listened to them with a sort of detached amusement, pretended to be in a bleak dystopian thriller.

Apparently Gord lost interest in our non-conversation, had already disappeared back behind the cubicle wall, most likely to look at porn or sports websites. They were kind of the same thing.

The Gord distraction had almost made me forget my existential crisis. Luckily, right on cue, a thick stack of reports landed on my desk with a comical thud.

"Thank...you..." I started to say, but the mysterious courier was already gone.

Waves of anxiety came rushing back. I felt sick to my stomach, on the verge of hyperventilating.

Where's the restroom, I thought. *I need to rest.*

Rising on wobbly legs, I moved away from my desk and headed down the neverending corridor of cubes. My vision became fuzzy. I moved past blobs and blurs, dodging distorted co-workers and other obstacles. Somehow, I reached the men's room. Locking myself in the least detestable stall I could find, I closed my eyes and tried to catch my breath, slow my rapidly beating heart. My hands began to tremble again, a tingly numb sensation overtaking them. I stretched my fingers in and out, making sure they were still there.

After a couple of minutes I was able to regain some composure. Took a deep breath and opened my eyes. Gagged. *When's the last time they cleaned this place?*

Emerging from the stall, I shuffled over to the sink, splashed cold water on my face. Stared at my porous skin and bloodshot eyes in the mirror.

Yep, everything was back to normal.

Back to work.

As I pushed through the door, I must have been feeling like myself, because my mind returned to the same irrational fear that plagued me each time I exited the men's room—that my zipper was down, penis out, flopping around for the entire office to see.

I looked down.

Okay, good. No penis flop.

(Note: Perhaps this flashback was a bad idea.)

Back in my cubicle, I grabbed the top sheet from the tower of reports and was off and running, typing and clicking my life away once again. If some impartial onlooker were observing me, they may have even assumed I gave two shits for Berger & Balki. But how could I? The only time I had any contact with the elusive partners was around Christmas time, through email well-wishes no doubt composed by a secretary.

To be fair, the secretary seemed nice.

There was the familiar crackle of the loudspeaker above me. Only this time, I stopped and looked up. It was my name blaring throughout the office floor.

"ART RICHARDSON, PLEASE REPORT TO YOUR SUPERVISOR IMMEDIATELY. THANK YOU."

I was flattered.

I was led down the corridor and into a meeting room I wasn't aware existed. Two neatly dressed older women sat at the head of the table, perfectly practiced smiles on their faces. One of them motioned for me to take a seat.

They were firing me.

I listened as they explained. They had surveillance footage of me talking on my cell phone during work hours. I stared across the table as they continued to speak, but soon my eyes began to wander, now really taking in the room. It was a nice room. Lots of leather-bound books, big fancy window overlooking the park. Even the table looked important.

The women had stopped talking. One of them pushed a paper across the table, along with a pen. There were some words on the paper that appeared as one big blur to me and a place for me to sign at the bottom. They sat, silently blinking. I pled my case. Told them that I was on my break at the time and that actually I had been speaking with my mechanic regarding an emergency car situation. This could have been true. Couldn't remember.

They told me I had broken company rules. That Berger & Balki & Associates had a zero-tolerance policy when it came to cell phone usage.

Apparently they were finished, because they stood up. Unsure of what else to do, I signed the paper. One of them snatched it up, informed me that I should gather my things and leave the building immediately. I didn't have any things.

Well, I had my lunch.

A gum-smacking Rent-A-Guard accompanied me to the break room to collect my brown bag. All eyes were on me as I marched past rows of cubicles, Gord getting in one last obnoxious grin at my expense. Then it was down to the main lobby, where my employee badge was confiscated and I was promptly cast out into the unknown.

It was all bullshit, of course. Only later did I learn of the company politics involved, the arbitrary reasons for getting rid of entry-level (see: expendable) employees such as myself. This is what the corporate world refers to as "turnover."

As I made my exit, an arm-flailing meltdown would have been entirely justified, even expected. Imagine the memorable witticisms and colorful curses I could have hurled at those spineless company imbeciles. No doubt it could have been a firing for the ages, a legend whispered among the other peons for years to come.

But a funny thing happened. As I stepped out of that building and into the sunlit city, I realized that I was suddenly a part of it all. That the sun was shining on me for once.

I felt like I was floating.

I didn't go home, not right away. Went across the street to the park, sat on some concrete steps in front of a large fountain. Stared down into the shallow coin-filled pool, at the blue chemical water, sounds of laughing children and muttering homeless people all around me.

Thought about jumping in. Didn't. Opened my lunch bag instead.

My afternoon sandwich had never tasted so good. I devoured it, relishing every bite, smacking my lips.

My gaze drifted upwards to the top of the spraying fountain of water, endlessly spouting into the air. Stubborn, persistent.

Sitting in the park that day, I knew I could never go back to my old life, to a boring job that I hated. No longer would I simply pass the days away until I die, wasting precious time and energy on things I was not passionate about.

But what would I do?

All of a sudden the answer seemed so clear, so simple.

Ever since I was a boy, I loved to read. Loved stories, dreamt of becoming a writer. Pages from books, to my youthful eyes, were so full of life, of endless possibilities.

So my days were mostly spent in my room, scribbling in marble-covered composition books. Creating my own worlds and escaping into them whenever I wanted. Whenever the other kids at school were going somewhere without me, whenever mom and dad were getting into one of their knockdown brawls. When I didn't fit in, which was most of the time.

When real life became too much, I had somewhere to go.

Always imagined becoming a professional author one day. Though whenever I mentioned this out loud, the general consensus was that such aspirations wouldn't get me anywhere except living in the streets.

Writing sort of fell to the wayside as my hormones took over and I discovered video games and comic books and books with naked people in them. There were the unremarkable, lackadaisical days of high school, college. Once I was done what was expected of me, I found myself in a post-education malaise, without drive or purpose, lost. Somehow, in the midst of this, I met an amazing woman named Laura, and we began a life together.

Shit, I thought, staring at the fountain. *What will Laura think of all this?*

Laura wants you to be happy.

But she works. Works hard. I should work too, earn an income. Contribute. Not chase some silly dream.

A career in writing wasn't feasible, wouldn't pay the bills.

But maybe that didn't need to matter anymore.

Look at that fountain. It's glorious. Look all around you. The world is full of possibilities. You are full of potential. And you've just been given a chance to realize it. To be happy.

Though it wasn't until a dinner party that everything really changed, when I truly took a leap into the unknown.

But let's save that for later. Space these flashbacks out a bit.

What am I, some kind of amateur?

EIGHT

The inside of a small shack full of art supplies came into focus, and I remembered where I was, what I was supposed to be doing.

You're supposed to be writing, Art.

I looked up from my desk and noticed that Tomas and Eve had returned from their filmmaking excursion. I also noticed—not without horror—that Eve's face and body were covered in blood.

"Jesus Christ," I said.

"Don't freak out." Eve used her arm to wipe some of the dark redness from her forehead. "I did it to myself."

"Oh, special effects."

"No. It's real. Stabbed myself in the hand with an X-ACTO knife. Smeared gore juice all over my body."

"And I filmed it." Tomas stepped out from behind her with a proud smile. "Looked badass."

Clorie had spun from her canvas to observe the madness. "Shit. Eve. Did you hit an artery?"

"I'm fine. Do it on stage all the time."

"I guess it's…a horror movie?" I ventured.

"Experimental film," said Eve.

"Psychological horror," said Tomas, at the same time.

"What?" Eve rounded to face him. "No. It's not a fucking dumbass horror shit movie. You shit."

"Thought I was a sheep."

"Sheep shit."

Clorie's eyes were wide, still taking in all the blood. "Looks pretty horrifying to me."

"Just wait till I add the sound effects and score. Throw in some sick jump scares. Ha. Gonna scare the shit out of you." Tomas was bobbing his head and dancing in place now. "No, but seriously. It will be so hype. But also deep and shit. The story, I mean. It's all an allegory. For something. You'll see."

"I can help with the score." Agony grabbed his acoustic guitar and came toward us, threatening us with his music again. "Check out this poem set to melody I just wrote."

Eve crossed her bloody arms. "You mean a song?"

Agony began to strum and croon painfully:

I'm angry as cupcakes,
happy as a stormy cloud—

Eve threw something. It narrowly missed Agony, smashed into the wall behind him.

"Hey, not cool!" Tomas ran to cradle the broken camera in his arms, looking back at Eve in disbelief. "You have any idea how expensive this thing is in real life?"

"Yeah, well this isn't real life, is it?"

"You probably damaged the footage we shot today!"

"So what. I didn't sign on to make a horror movie. The *director* misled me."

"Whatever. I'll shoot it again! On film this time! As soon as I...figure out how to do that."

"Maybe Leonard can help you." Clorie looked around. "Hey, where is the old head anyway?"

Agony was gazing out a window. "It's getting dark."

A few minutes later, the door of the shack swung open and Leonard entered shivering, carrying two large buckets of water. "Whew! Still colder than a witch's tit, in case anyone was wondering. Anyway, I was able to find a stream, but no edible berries. And as far as the crops go..." He shook his head, biting his lip. "None of it looks ripe enough to eat. Perhaps it's off-season? ...do farms have off-seasons? Either way, we're basically fucked." He set down the buckets and scratched the top of his wrinkled dome. "I'll be honest, folks. There's a strong possibility we're going to have to eat one of those animals soon. Hope no one here is a vegetarian."

"Chickens lay eggs," Eve pointed out.

"Right! That's an idea, yes."

"Um. I'm vegan." Clorie looked around at us. "Well, I was thinking about becoming vegan, before I came here…"

"Yeah, you might want to put that on hold a bit longer…"

"It's okay," said Agony. "Let's be hungry. Let's, like, *use* the hunger."

Guess Agony was out of candy bars.

Eve shot an evil glare in Agony's direction. "I'll use your ass for a hat."

"What?"

"Ass hat."

The hunger was getting to us.

After more bickering, we came to the conclusion that keeping ourselves alive would help with the whole "creating" thing. Also the whole "living" thing.

First food, then work.

About that cow slaughtering. It happened.

To decide who would perform the ritual sacrifice, an intense rock-paper-scissors tournament was held. Tomas and Agony lost and so went on to the prestigious main event: The Flipping of the Leaf. Each person had to call it in the air and whomever's leaf side landed facing up had to do the slaughtering.

"Reddish-yellow!"

"Yellowy-green-brown!"

It was windy that day, so it took the leaf a long time to fall. The suspense was brutal.

"Fuck, man." Tomas stared down at the reddish-yellow side of the fallen frond, his shoulders slouched in defeat. "I don't want to do it."

"The Great Leaf has foretold," I said.

"Sorry, brother." Leonard put his hand on Tomas' shoulder. "Them's the rules."

Eve grunted, pushing herself up from the log she was sitting on. "Psh. Rules. What a bunch of sheep."

Clorie was shaking her head. "Hold on. With no one to tend to the animals…they're probably going to die soon anyway. Which is sad. But, convenient? I say we wait till they keel over."

"Fuck this." Eve brandished her trusty X-ACTO knife. "You pussies wait here. Mama's gonna bring back dinner."

She spat on the ground and walked off, disappearing over a small hill as the rest of us looked on.

"Why do I feel like this is about to turn into a scene from *Apocalypse Now*?"

Sadly, my reference fell on deaf ears. I turned to Tomas.

"Oh, come on. You've at least seen *Apocalypse Now*."

"Nah."

"Not even in film school?"

"Nope."

The horror…

Agony cleared his throat and said something oddly logical.

"We could try fishing."

That was when we heard the rallying cry off in the distance. Our backs stiffened. What ensued was nothing short of a massacre. We couldn't see anything, but we certainly heard it. Screeching and grunting and what I imagine was lots of violent stabbing. None of it sounded like the beautiful and respectful ritual we were all envisioning.

This was no sacrifice to the lords of whatever.

It was murder.

The only sound more sickening: our stomachs rumbling in anticipation.

NINE

The makeshift spit roast turned slowly. We sat around the campfire watching, salivating like a pack of rabid dogs. Then, in the lingering light of dusk, we chewed, tore, sawed with crude instruments. Nothing had ever tasted so good and so wrong at the same time.

Amid the chorus of lip smacking, I paused to take a breath and to watch my fellow cave people pull at charred flesh with bare hands and teeth. There were specks of blood on their legs and arms, juices running down their faces and necks. Eve, true to form, was the most disturbing and messiest of all. She was moaning and grunting, savoring her kill, new blood mixing with the old.

It was a grisly scene, folks.

Clorie gulped down another mound of meat, a veil of queasiness coming over her. "Think I'm gonna puke."

"So good," Tomas muttered, tearing skin with his teeth. Raw gooeyness leaked from his lips, down his neck.

Leonard stood, wiping his mouth with the back of his hand.

"Well. Now that we have some food in our bellies—thanks to the lovely and voracious Eve—let's go around and tell each other what we worked on today." He sat back down with a dopey grin on his face, apparently opening the floor.

Eve stood first, thrusting a large bone into the air.

"Cunt dick," she said. Sat back down.

We all nodded.

Agony got up next, scratching the back of his head. "Well, I wrote five and a half poems today. Here's one." He cleared his throat, holding his notebook out in front of him. "It's called, *The Days of the Week are Bullshit*."

He recited:

> *Monday. Bullshit.*
> *Tuesday. Bullshit.*
> *Wednesday. Bullshit.*
> *Thursday. Thursday's all right.*
> *Friday. Bullshit.*
> *Saturday. Bullshit.*
> *Fuckday.*
> *Fuck you, dad.*

He closed the notebook and sat down, nodding to himself. The group snapped their fingers in mock or possibly sincere beatnik fashion.

"Nice work, Agony." Leonard turned to the next victim. "How 'bout you, Tomas?"

Tomas jumped up, bobbing back and forth excitedly.

"Okay, okay. So, I realized something today. I want to make feel-good movies. Want people to feel good. Life's so short. Filled with pain. Anger. Disappointment. Look at Eve. She's fucked up! I don't want to fuck people up anymore. My movies will be positive. Pure entertainment!"

"Entertainment is good," I said. "Makes you forget about death for a few seconds."

Eve cupped her hands around her mouth. "Booo, sit down."

"And you know what," Tomas continued, "Clorie was right, about violence being a crutch. There's enough of that in the world. We need more positivity. No more violence in my films."

Leonard raised an eyebrow. "You have a new film brewin', brother?"

Tomas' eyes widened. "Yes. It's called *The Grilldown*." He looked around at the circle of puzzled faces in the light of the fire. "Picture it, my friends: A beautiful summer day. Bunch of bros and their respective lady friends hangin' out at the local pool. Having a BBQ. Some brews. Splashin' around. Having a good time, you know."

Tomas demonstrated tilting a can of beer to his mouth and grooving to some tunes. I appreciated the pantomime, but still wasn't quite getting it.

We all waited for him to continue as he stood there, grinning at us.

I leaned forward. "All right, and…"

"And that's it."

"That's it?" I said. "They just…hang out?"

Clorie furrowed her brow. "Well, something should happen, right? Like maybe one of the characters is going through some personal stuff. Or there's an accident or something?"

"What?" Tomas looked almost offended. "No. No-no. See, that's the thing. They just *chill*. That's it. Drink beers, hang out. Play grab-ass, throw each other in the pool. Maybe some square in a business suit shows up, gets thrown in the pool."

Leonard nodded, offering an encouraging smile. "Uh. Cool. Sounds like a blast."

Eve blew a raspberry. "Sounds like the dumbest piece of dogshit I've ever heard."

"For ninety minutes?" I still wasn't getting it.

"Constructive feedback," Leonard reminded.

Agony paused from swatting at a buzzing insect to ask, "Are there dope jams at the party?"

"Oh, no doubt," Tomas assured. "Soundtrack is gonna be a real banger."

Clorie shrugged. "Maybe it's a musical?"

"Yes!"

"And the main character gets a *new grill*!" Leonard suggested. "One that is much better than his old grill!"

Tomas shook his head. "No. No main character, no plot. Nothin' but grillin' and chillin'."

"This may actually be the most experimental film ever made," I said.

"Yeah." Eve snorted. "Submit that shit to Cannes, you dweeb. I'm sure you'll grab top prize."

Tomas lost his cool, shouting above the flames, *"Maybe I will!"*

"Hey now." Leonard tried to ease the tension. "We have to support one another's ideas, not tare them down. Tomas, *The Grilldown* sounds like a blast. I'll be first in line to see it."

"Thank you." Tomas bowed graciously, sat down.

"Um." Clorie got up slowly. "Not sure I can top that but...this is what I made today." She lifted a canvas and held it in front of her, displaying a landscape of murky smears and blotches. So this was what she had been working on. It was really something. The more I stared at it, the more there was to see. It had a surreal beauty, a mesmerizing quality, instantly drawing me into its dark world.

"Looks like my beer shits," said Eve.

"Thank you." Clorie lowered the canvas, quickly sat back down.

"I like it." Leonard nodded at her. "Fine work, Clorie."

Tomas squinted at the painting like he was trying to solve a math problem. "Freaky. What does it represent?"

Eve scoffed loudly. "You're not supposed to ask that."

"No, it's okay..." Clorie gazed at her creation. "There's a lot of...rage in this piece. You can see my anger in the erratic strokes, choice of watercolors." She looked back at us. "Well, that's only in hindsight. It's not really a conscious thing."

"Why were you so pissed off?" Tomas asked. "Someone back home? ...girlfriend, maybe? You swing both ways, right?"

Clorie made a face.

Eve chimed in. "Stop asking ignorant questions, ya butt sucker."

"Butt su—? Wha—I...I can ask whatever I want! Plus, you ruined my film, Eve. So I have nothing to show, thanks to you."

"So what. This isn't 'show-and-tell.'"

"Eve is right," said Leonard. "Showing what we've made is great, but we'll have plenty of time for that once we return home. Hell, then we can show everybody! Right now let's focus on inspiration, ideas, keep the momentum going."

He turned to me. "Art. My fellow author. Tell us about your plans for your novel."

"Um. Plans?"

"Yeah. Saw you jotting something down in your little notebook earlier…the words must have begun to flow." Leonard leaned in, the glow from the campfire on his face. "Tell us about the words, brother."

"Right. The words. The words were, um…words?" I laughed awkwardly, scratched the back of my head. "Still figuring it out, I guess."

"Hey, that's okay. The words are there, trust me. All you need to do is snatch them up and write them down. Then you can do whatever you want with 'em! Chop 'em up, throw 'em in the air. See what happens. Like all those beat losers used to do."

"Right."

"You'll get there, man. Hell. It's only Day One."

"Uh, thanks."

"This is lame." Eve kicked a large rock in Leonard's direction. "I killed a cow. That was my art for today, and none of you dick-bags even attended." Then she added in a mocking voice, "Oh, but let's all be super supportive of the wimpy writer, who's obviously never written anything in his life."

Damn. "Hey. I've put pen to paper…"

"Yeah. But have you, like, *written* anything?"

"Sure I have. I'm just…I have writer's block, at the moment. That's all."

Eve folded her bloodstained arms and leaned back against a log. "Sure, whatever you say, butt paste." At least this was one of her more interesting insults. Wasn't even sure what it meant.

(Note: Research butt paste.)

"It's fine." I scratched the back of my head, stared down at the dirt. "The novel as an art form is dead anyway. Attention spans, and all. Maybe I should focus on writing short stories. Real simple, slice of life type stuff."

"Raymond Carver over here." Leonard snorted, thumbing in my direction.

I turned to him with a big fake smile. "Excellent reference, Leonard. And he didn't even write about robots *or* aliens!"

Tomas was squinting at me now. "What's your last name again?"

"Um. Richardson."

He shook his head. "You should change it to something that pops more. Will help you stand out, sell more books."

"My name?"

"A pen name isn't a bad idea," Leonard agreed.

"Is this really what we should be talking about?" I asked.

"Last name should be something cool," said Tomas. "Like Zaxx or Zapp. Something with a Z."

Stantz has a Z in it. Wonder if that's even Leonard's real name.

I noticed that Clorie was looking at me, scrunching her face. "So you…don't know what kind of story you want to write? Like, at all?"

"Well…not entirely." I cleared my throat. "Just want to make sure it feels right, you know? Want it to be…genuine."

Everyone got quiet. Evidently this statement struck a chord.

Then Eve did what she normally did, broke the silence with her own brand of statement. Threw her arms in the air, shouting, "We're all just awful broken flesh-machines!"

Agony nodded, staring off. "Deep."

Leonard smirked. "Hey. That's a good title for your novel, Art. Sounds literary."

Fuck you, Leonard. Think you're so much better than me. With your stupid Z in your stupid made-up name.

"I gotta pee," I said.

Leaving the campfire, I wandered away from the group and the Art Shack (as we now called it). Ambled down a slope toward some trees.

Crickets serenaded me as I sighed, streamed urine into plants. Then I noticed something deeper off in the woods.

Another shack.

It was mostly obscured by trees, but it seemed bigger than the Art Shack. And it was lit up inside, like there was a party going on.

I zipped up and called out, "Hey guys."

Inside the newly discovered shack, we stood blinking in unison at the veritable feast before us.

Yes, *food*.

Impossibly long tables of fresh fruits and vegetables, tantalizing meats, decadent desserts. Whoever set it up had clearly gone out of their way to make everything look as enticing as possible. The thing was, we would have gladly devoured diseased horse shlong no more than thirty minutes ago.

And yet here was this wondrous array of ready-made food, all for us. I nearly wept.

Agony was the first to regain the ability of speech.

"Nachos!"

"Chimichangas and churros!" shouted Tomas. "Tacos and fajitas!"

We noticed the banner on the wall: "Taco Tuesday."

"Ooo," we collectively cooed.

Leonard moved toward one of the tables for closer inspection.

"Food's hot. Where the hell are they cooking it?"

Clorie was looking around with a bewildered expression on her face.

"*Who* the hell is cooking it?"

"Who cares?" Tomas shrugged. "It's food."

I scratched my chin, gazing around at the glorious unexpected banquet. "Man," I said. "Wish we had discovered this before we killed and ate that cow…"

The group turned, frowning.

Well. Someone had to say it.

"*I* killed the cow," Eve reminded.

Leonard turned back to the spread. "I'm beginning to think there's a lot about this place we don't know."

Agony stepped beside him. "Maybe we are supposed to keep discovering things," he said, looking back at us. "Like, it's all part of the experience…part of the point."

I looked at him. "Discovering shacks with stuff in them is part of the point?"

"Yeah, man. This is all definitely part of the point of the whole thing."

"We should stop talking about the point," Clorie said. "The point is not the point."

"Right on." Agony nodded.

While the rest of the group continued to debate the appearance of this new shack with its smorgasbord of food, I grabbed a plate and dug in, taking sample bites of anything within reach. Feeling everyone's eyes on me, I glanced up. "Didn't fill up too much on cow earlier…" I uttered between inhaling bits of other animals.

The others must have had room left in their bellies as well. Soon we were all at the tables, stuffing our faces.

Even Eve gave in to the herd mentality this time. Went straight for dessert, stacking cream-filled cookies on her plate. Despite this, she still managed to bring the mood down with a typically depressing observation.

"We're sad predictable creatures, doomed to repeat the same patterns over and over," she said, cramming cookies into her mouth. "That's why life has to end, so we don't get stuck in the same fucking loop for all of eternity."

"Heavy." Agony lowered his plate for a moment. "Like some Bill Murray *Groundhog Day* shit."

"Wow." Clorie pointed. "They even have refrigerators plugged in over there."

"And a grill," I noticed. "We can have our own grilldown." I looked across the table at Tomas. "That title's really growing on me, by the way. Have you considered trademarking it?"

"Good idea, bro," Tomas said as he stuffed the pockets of his shorts with churros.

Agony eyed the big juicy steaks on display, drooling. This was fancy stuff. Not that barbaric, grisly crap we had gnawed around the campfire. He forked a piece of meat and began to lift it before noticing me watching. Was that a flicker of shame I saw?

"Um. I guess we could still use the fire for like…S'mores?"

"We *could*…" I said. "Though microwaved S'mores taste pretty much the same."

"Yeah, good point…"

Eventually we moved to sit and eat at one of the smaller tables, a custom we vaguely remembered from civilization. As I gorged—binging, anticipating the inevitable purge—I noticed something out the window. A vaguely human shape standing on a hill in the distance, outlined in sparse moonlight. The figure appeared to be facing the shack, indeed seemed to be staring at us. At me.

This was alarming. Frightening, even. I may have even screamed if my mouth wasn't full of burrito.

After finishing and thoroughly licking my fingers, my gaze returned to the hilltop. The dark figure was gone. Only the moon, eerily looming in the night sky, gazed back.

I looked around at the others, happily chomping and chewing. No one seemed to notice anything, so I decided to drop it. Grabbed an empanada.

TEN

Morning arrived, bringing with it bright blue sky and some wicked indigestion.

I surveyed the campsite. Everyone was beginning to wake. Everyone except Eve, who was MIA. I figured she likely ventured off to kill more animals—for fun this time. Bunnies, perhaps.

The others rose with hands on stomachs, wincing. Still, there were satisfied smiles behind those pained expressions. At least until they ran to nearby bushes, squatting and moaning.

My own stomach was rumbling. I gave it a pat, fondly remembering the delicious food binge from the night before. Sure, my tummy ached, but at least it was full.

Clorie came back to the campsite, wiping her mouth. Stood staring vacantly at the ashes of last night's fire.

"Has anyone seen...anyone?"

In the distance a sheep baaed.

"Huh?" Leonard paused from combing his beard with a twig.

"People," she said. "Other people. Farm workers, caretakers..."

"Now, Clorie. We can't allow ourselves to become distracted by such unexplained mysteries." Leonard pulled a black beetle-looking thing from his gray whiskers, held it between his fingers to examine it. "Remember what we talked about? We're here to create. Not question."

A cow mooed.

Clorie bit her lip, looked away.

It was only natural to have questions, to want to learn more about the farm. And it was indeed frustrating that each new discovery only led to more questions. But I reminded myself that none of it really mattered.

As Clorie herself had said—*the point is not the point.*

Not worrying about things was new for me, but I was getting used to it. The duties and rituals of daily life were already melting away, becoming a thing of the past. The very concept of time now seemed preposterous to me.

But there were still remnants of my old life that tried to break through, tried to intrude. Persistent, bothersome thoughts.

As I gazed over at Clorie, I saw another face. My wife Laura. I missed her, I remembered. Missed my dog.

Well. I'd be back before they knew it. It was for the good of the family. Daddy had to venture out on his own. Needed to grow, flourish. To become an artist, a better person.

They would thank me when I returned.

Well, my dog would probably lick me.

Maybe my wife would lick me too. Who knew. Things were changing.

A rooster crowed.

Leonard stood. Hands on his hips, he stretched a leg on top of a large rock, trying his best to look like an adventurer on the cover of a pulp novel.

"Let us start our art," he said.

It appeared the art had started without us.

Upon entering the Art Shack, we found Eve. The thing is, she was dead.

At least it sure looked that way. She lay sprawled among scattered supplies, on top of a large silk canvas splattered with crimson. There were bruises covering her pale skin, rainbows of purple and red to match her hair.

We stood around, looking down at her.

I wanted to scream. *Should I scream?*

"So *this* is her performance art," Agony said. His gaze slowly drifted, peering up at us. "Right?"

Tomas looked up as well. "She did seem to like to hurt herself."

My eyes met theirs. "You think Eve killed herself...as an art piece?"

Tomas glanced down at her again. "You think she's dead?"

"Seems that way." Leonard nodded. "Yes. I'd say she's almost certainly dead."

Tomas scratched the top of his head. "I don't know, man. Eve was pretty weird, and kind of a bitch. Just saying. She might be faking, to try and get a reaction or something..."

I considered this before shaking my head. "I doubt she'd care enough to go to these lengths. Her disdain for us was fairly obvious."

"Unless her whole *thing* was an act!"

"What thing?"

"Her thing. The way she acted. And stuff."

"Like, her whole life was performance art?"

"Yeah! Maybe. She was fucking weird."

"Maybe it was food poisoning," said Agony. "From last night."

"That's some violent food poisoning," said Leonard.

This whole time Clorie had been completely silent, her eyes never leaving Eve's body. When she finally spoke, it came out in a tremble.

"Guys. She's fucking dead."

A heavy stillness set in. We rejoined her, gazing down upon our lost little Eve. The blood and the colors and the violence of it all.

She would never spit another loogie, never call anyone "butt paste" ever again, our Eve.

Eve-Tron, I thought. *That's what she had wanted us to call her.*

A yelp escaped Clorie's lips. She covered her mouth, ran straight out of the shack. We stood there, listening to her heaving bile into the grass between sobs.

My stomach grumbled.

Shock aside, I was pretty hungry.

Would it be Pancake Day? Today felt like a Pancake Day.

ELEVEN

There were no pancakes.

There were, however, eggs. Eggs benedict alongside Belgian waffles drenched in butter and syrup, with hash browns and a zesty orange slice. It would have to do for now.

We sat around one of the tables inside the Eat Shack (that's what we were calling this one). No one besides me had touched their breakfast. Instead my cohorts were busy discussing Eve, the possible circumstances surrounding her fate.

There was the "last performance" idea, which had some credence to it. Eve hated the world and the people in it. Her suicide may have been her final statement on the matter.

However, the prevailing—and much more dangerous and exciting theory —was that Eve had been murdered.

And if that was the case, who dun it?

I buttered my waffle, eyeing Tomas at the end of the table. Tomas loathed Eve, but was he capable of murder? Hell, he could barely operate a camera.

We proceeded to play detective, discussing the scene of the crime, calling on all of the cop movies, the episodes of *Law & Order* we had collectively absorbed.

Clorie shook her head, her face drained and sullen. "So this retreat has turned into a murder mystery. How lame."

Leonard scratched his chin before pushing his glasses back into place. "Let's think outside the box here. Be creative. That's what we do, right? Perhaps there's more of an…otherworldly, fantastical explanation to all this."

I rolled my eyes. "That's creative, all right."

Leonard dropped his fork, spun to face me. "Well, how about you, Mr. Literature? What do you think happened? Something *literary*, no doubt."

"I'm still not sure what that means, Leonard. Anyway, I'm in the same boat as all of you. Didn't hear or see anything."

Leonard squinted, scanning the faces at the table. "Unless someone *did* hear or see something, *knows* something, and is keeping quiet."

A loud crunch turned everyone's heads. We watched Agony take a bite of toast, followed by some equally noisy chewing.

There was no way Agony knew something. I was pretty sure he didn't know anything. Like, at all.

Clorie sighed and stared down into her mug. "Being antagonistic and blindly accusing people isn't going to get us anywhere. We need to think rationally."

"Oh, I'm thinking rationally all right." Leonard tapped his wrinkled dome. "I got a real rational brain."

"Uh-huh." Clorie rolled her eyes before returning to her steaming morning coffee. Shit, *coffee*. We had coffee now. Had almost hugged the coffeemaker when I first saw it. Fine stuff, too. Beans must have been straight from Venezuela or some shit. Though really, could have come from anywhere. Nothing was labeled.

Clorie slid her chair back, stood up. Another wave of nausea must have hit, because she quickly turned and made her way out of the Eat Shack.

Looking around at the others, selfishly eating and drinking delicious coffee, I knew I had to be the one to console poor Clorie.

So I excused myself, burped, excused myself again, and followed her outside.

I found Clorie sitting by the edge of a stream, amongst wildflowers and other flowers I imagined were wild as well. The weather had become milder, but it brought with it a certain eerie stillness. This may have also had something to do with the corpse inside the Art Shack, but I tried to put that thought out of my mind. Instead, I thought about Clorie. How beautiful she looked, sitting there, her dark hair shimmering in the morning sunlight, gazing out over the trickling water.

"Hey."

She looked up at me.

"This is all pretty fucked up, huh?"

I said this in the hopes of making her smile, but her face remained frozen.

I tried again.

"You know, Eve was—"

"I don't want to talk about Eve."

"Oh. Sure."

I settled down in the grass beside her.

Clorie returned her gaze forward, looking out over the stream.

"I'm not thinking about what happened," she said.

"Okay. Good."

"I can't. I'm still trying to wrap my head around the fact that we're really here. Like, we actually did it. All of us. We came here."

She continued looking at the water. I continued looking at her.

"I think," she said, "this was my way of deciding, once and for all, if I could do this."

"What do you mean?"

"I mean…if I could pull it off. Dedicate my life to my craft, to the only thing I've ever wanted to do. Be able to live off of my work. But even after making it this far, the same questions come back. What if I'm not good enough? What if no one cares about my work? If the whole thing goes nowhere? I shouldn't think like that, but I can't help it." She sniffled. "I worry I fear failure too much."

"Hitler was a failed painter."

Again, trying to cheer her up.

I attempted to salvage it.

"...and look at what he accomplished."

Okay, let's abandon this particular analogy.

"Umm. You'll be fine."

"Thanks, Art." She tried to smile at me. "It's just...you ever worry that maybe there's too much shit in the world as it is? Are we only adding to all the noise?"

"Why even create, you mean?"

"Right."

"Hmm. Well, I—"

"Can I tell you something?"

You love me?

"Sure," I said.

"I was anorexic," she said. "I'm not anymore. But it's a struggle."

"Hmm. Agony was half-right."

"Fuck Agony. He's an asshole. But yeah, he was sort of right. About that."

"He's mostly just dumb."

We sat there listening to the water for a bit before she spoke again.

"I've had a pretty rough life."

I slapped a bug, smeared its guts on my arm. *Fuck you Thing That's Different From Me.*

"I'm sorry," I said to Clorie.

"Yeah. Well, I have."

"'Cause of the anorexia?"

"That's part of it..."

"The ex-boyfriend who used to make you blow on him...or did he blow you...?"

"Lots of shit, okay?"

"Gotcha."

"The point is, I've had a rough go of it. But who hasn't, right? I mean, things aren't easy for anyone. And dedicating your life to art doesn't exactly make it easier. Makes you crazy." She gazed around at the farm. "Maybe that's why all of us ended up here."

"We're artists, Clorie. Who knows why we do what we do? We can question it till the cows come home. But don't forget what you said: the point is not the point."

"...I said that?"

"Yeah."

"Hmm. Sounds like something an artsy person would say. Ha." She sniffed again, wiped her nose with the side of her hand. "Anyway. Enough of my shit...what about you? What kind of shit do you come from?"

"Huh?"

"Like, what kind of life did you leave to come here? You mentioned a wife..."

Did I?

"Yeah..."

I kept looking at her. Then, I did something crazy. Something Old Me would have shit himself at the mere thought of. I reached out and took Clorie's hand.

She turned to me. Looking into her eyes, I said, "We're all a little scared right now. None of us knows where we are, what's going to happen. But we're all in this together. And I'm here for you." I gave her soft hand a firm squeeze.

Clorie reached out with her other hand, unzipped my pants.

"Uhh," I said.

She lowered her head down to my crotch, blew on it with her mouth. Allowed herself to fall back onto the dewy grass with a wet thud before propping herself up on her elbows.

"Now do me," she said.

I grunted in breathless agreement, got on my knees in front of her. Staring into her sex, I decided I should come clean.

"I'm married," I said.

"I know."

"Oh yeah."

"Shut up and blow."

I did as I was told. Licked my lips, let flow a mighty blow. Followed with a few light, sensual ones for good measure.

"Oh, yeah," she said.

"Oh yeah?"

I'm having an affair. Wow. I'm such a cool person now.

She moaned loudly before abruptly leaning forward, pushing me back onto the grass. I stared up at the sky. The clouds looked like impressionistic blotches, something Clorie might paint. She was such a great artist. I envied her. Wanted to be her and inside her at the same time.

Clorie got on her knees and gripped my head, rubbed it on the crotch of her jeans. She groaned, writhing against my greasy dome. After a full minute of this, she kicked off her shoes and smashed her feet into my face. I started to kiss her toes. She yelled "No," so I stopped, continued to let her bare feet ram into my face and mouth. Then she grabbed my shoulders, pulled me to a standing position. Got down on her knees, head-butted my groin.

"Ow."

"Shut up."

"Okay."

She started rubbing her head on the thin fabric covering my genitals, like a cat finding a comfy new resting place, until I felt like I wasn't going to be able to stand it anymore.

"Should I, should we—" I started to unbuckle my belt.

"No, fuck. No."

Clorie stood, let out a shriek. She ran, headed toward the Art Shack.

Dazed, I got to my feet. Pants still unzipped, sagging, I hobbled after her. There was an uncontrollable urge within my body. I forgot everything else, all the reasons I was there. Art be damned.

I shuffled like a zombie to the window of the shack, pressed myself up against the glass, peered inside. Saw Clorie painting. Painting hard. Eve's body was still there, still dead.

Clorie splattered the canvas. Forceful, chaotic brushstrokes. Using her toes, her face, her hair. Whipping her hair around, paint flying. Dipping her hand in the paint, smearing it onto the canvas. Moaning, dipping her hand into Eve's still-wet blood, splashing some of that onto the canvas as well. She was panting now, reaching some sort of climax. With one last scream she leaped into the canvas, trying to become one with it, to swim inside her own creation.

This was either an act of intense inspiration or the most animated orgasm I had ever seen. Maybe it was both. There was paint everywhere.

"Oh shit oh fuck."

My breath fogged up the glass and I slumped down onto the grass, spent.

Reaching into my coat pocket, I pulled out a matchbook and a pack of cigarettes. Along with the art supplies and food, the farm was even providing us deadly vices such as these.

I puffed one, satisfied. Had never inhaled smoke from a cigarette before.

I coughed a lot.

Felt good.

TWELVE

The next day Eve's body was gone.

Strange. But then, so was everything else.

Anyway, it spared us the stench of a rotting corpse, disposing of said corpse.

Someone suggested a sort of "mock funeral" for our departed sister. That seemed fitting, since Eve would have certainly mocked the very idea of a funeral.

So, that's what we did.

Although for a group of creative people, we were unable to come up with much in the way of a grave marker. Eventually we settled on one long stick in the ground.

This was no puny twig, mind you. It was a stick of respectable caliber and thickness. A proper, dignified stick, representing a certain stark solemnness. Or solemn starkness.

True, we could have added an additional stick crosswise—but the consensus was that the gesture would not have been much appreciated by our fallen sister. Also, fuck symbols man.

Once the sun had fully risen, we sat in an open field in front of our makeshift memorial. It really was a nice-looking stick when one looked at it long enough. We had chosen some nice land to stick the stick into, as well. No dirt, only grass. Only the best for Eve.

Before the formalities were to begin, Tomas walked over with a steaming mug in his hand, bent down to whisper something to me.

"Have you tried the coffee today? Fresh as shit, bro. Fucking delicious coffee."

I told him that yes, I had tried the coffee and that indeed it was fucking delicious. Even better than the day before. Where did they get their beans?

"Probably Venezuela or some shit," he said, went to take his seat.

We all waited for the ceremony to begin, whatever it was going to be.

Agony got up and walked over to the stick, turned to face the yawning audience. He cleared his throat and commenced what I suppose was a eulogy.

"Eve…Eve was a good one," he began.

I nodded solemnly, remembering the wet sting of her spit in my face.

"I didn't have the privilege of her company for very long…but one thing I learned about Eve, is that she loved to laugh."

A soft whimper came from Tomas' direction, and I saw Leonard lean over to console him. Must have spilled his coffee.

I glanced sideways at Clorie, seated next to me. She was staring down at the grass between her feet, her body stiff.

Turning toward her, I pointed at a dark mole on my arm, whispered, "Ever notice this before?"

"Um. No. But I don't, like, look at your body."

"…think it's cancer?"

"Everything's cancer."

Agony was still talking.

"'We're all just awful broken flesh machines'…Eve said that once. Being a poet, in tune with beautiful words, I was stunned by the beauty of those words. Stunned. Like, wow. Really deep shit. Crazy. But that was Eve. You know?"

Had Eve actually said that? Sounded like something she would say. I do remember her using the words "cunt dick" and "butt paste."

Agony started to veer off a bit at this point, rambling, going on some sort of monologue about his depressing childhood, how his father never respected him.

"My dad always told me I was a fuckup…that I'd never amount to anything…"

I leaned over to Clorie. "Think he'll come back around to Eve?"

Clorie sniffled, wiped her eye. "I...I think I loved her," she whispered, staring at the stick.

In the days that followed, the image of Eve's body in the Art Shack seemed more and more like a dream. With no answers or leads—and no way to leave—we resigned to putting the half-assed investigation on hold.

Instead focused on salvaging what remained of our time on the farm. Remembered we were on a farm. That there were farm-things, animals.

In this spirit, I stopped by the pens now and then to fraternize with the livestock. Sometimes this included Agony.

Found him there one time, sitting cross-legged in the dirt, staring intensely, attempting to create some kind of mental bridge between him and a chicken.

Plopping down beside him, I joined in, stared at the chicken as well. The chicken was not very good at staring back. Its head bobbed erratically, turning this way and that, wings fluttering.

Still, Agony seemed determined to bond with his new feathered friend. Keeping his eyes on the chicken, he said, "I live each day to die at night."

I let this linger in the foul-smelling air before responding.

"Poem or song lyrics?"

"Not sure yet."

I stared at Agony staring at the chicken.

Perhaps this was normal for him. His way of attempting to push the still-fresh image of a dead young woman from his mind. Shoo, troubling image.

I pointed at the bird, pecking its feathers now.

"Are you attempting to do an Energy Poem with that chicken?"

"No, man." Agony remained still, his brow furrowed in deep contemplation. "Well, kinda. Mostly I'm observing."

"Life."

"Life in motion."

"Hmm. Isn't life always in motion?"

"Whoa..."

Agony reminded me of myself in my early twenties. My pseudo-philosophical phase. Reading books that I thought were really "deep," hoping they would provide all the answers. This was back when I was always looking for the point in things. I needed answers, was obsessed with finding them. Thought they were perhaps hidden within *Siddhartha*, that book I thought was a genuine Buddhist artifact but turned out to be a novel written by some German dude. Man. What a crock.

A fly landed on Agony's eyelid.

He said, "It's okay to cry, you know."

"All right."

"About Eve. And stuff. Noticed you holding back at the funeral…"

"Uh huh."

"You're among friends. We are all bonded."

"The chicken too?"

"Sure, all of us. Let it out, man."

"Thanks, Agony. I'll let you know if I feel anything coming on."

"Right on."

I glanced over at him. "…do you want to cry?"

Agony swallowed, allowing for a dramatic pause before he spoke again.

"Angels weep…when I cry."

I nodded, unsure if this was one of those things Agony said that sounded deep but actually meant nothing.

"…come on. SOUND DUNGEON lyrics. 'Angel Tears in Hell.' It was our biggest song."

"Uh, right." I looked at the chicken again. "Well, how's the observing going? Feeling anything?"

"Something, maybe. A truth."

"Don't leave me hangin'."

Agony's focus finally wavered, drifted upwards. He gazed at the sky, mouth open.

"I'm hungry," he said.

"Me too. Wonder what's for lunch."

A bug flew into Agony's mouth.

I stood, decided I would head over to the Eat Shack. Noticed Tomas was in the pen as well. He was sitting in the dirt with a camera, filming himself feeding a pig a doughnut.

"Hey man." I walked over to him. "Those doughnuts are keeping us alive."

"Sorry, bro. Pig looked hungry."

"Don't pigs eat slop?"

"You see any slop around here?" Tomas lowered his camera and looked up at me. "We got plenty of food. Gotta give back, bro. Circle of life."

They must have shown him *The Lion King* in film school.

"So, you're really going to dedicate your life to making feel-good popcorn flicks like *The Grilldown*?"

Tomas shrugged. "I want to focus on positivity, good vibes. The world has enough negativity, cynicism. That was Eve in a nutshell, and look at how she ended up."

"Dead."

"Exactly."

"I guess I can see what you mean."

He looked back at the monitor of his camera and zoomed in, focusing on a pebble in the dirt. "Can't wait to get back to some Wi-Fi. Start spreading my new message, post some inspiring shit to all my followers. Miss the Internet, bro. Being connected."

"You do?" Sometimes I forgot how young Tomas was. He'd basically lived his entire life online. Personally, I felt nothing but anxiety when it came to social media. Liked to pretend the Internet didn't exist. Except for looking up necessary things, like directions or porn.

"Yeah, bro. How am I supposed to tell everyone how I feel about stuff all the time?"

Gave this a moment to make sure he was serious. He was.

"Um. Don't know, man..."

A disturbing vision entered my mind: Tomas standing at a podium, behind him the backdrop of some glitzy award show. Giving a speech, talking about how thankful he is for all his success.

Accepting an award for his breakthrough film; a boring, belabored, overly serious metaphor for life. A film that ends with a magical CGI butterfly floating by the camera at the exact moment we're supposed to realize an inspiring message. The industry hails him as a true original, a bright young visionary poised to take Hollywood by storm.

Liquid-hot hate filled my being.

Fuck everyone and everything and all the assholes in-between.

I clenched my fist and looked at his youthful, objectively handsome face, wanting very much to punch it.

He doesn't deserve to be here. He doesn't understand.

I heard a squeal followed by some rustling in the dirt. Turned to see Agony attempting to mount one of the pigs—to ride it, I hoped.

I called over to him. "Gave up on the observing?"

Agony struggled to hold on. "This big guy looked like he wanted to have some fun. Didn't ya, boy?"

Didn't look too fun for the animal. The hog was bucking around, making ungodly noises, trying to knock the idiotic human off of him.

I heard some garbled snorting next to me. Turned my head to see Tomas filming himself once again shoving a donut into his pig's face.

Decided this was a good time to leave them to...whatever it was they were doing.

"Keep up the good work over here, fellas."

My novel was no closer to being finished (or begun, for that matter). But I sensed it brewing, percolating. Like the fine coffee with those sensational beans.

In the meantime, I joined my cohorts in enjoying the beautiful surroundings of the farm. Going on hikes, taking in the sights. Doing things, learning things. Things we never would have thought of doing before. Milking cows, tending chickens, moving bales of hay on top of other bales of hay, finding the best way to defecate in a hole without falling in. Practical things, important things.

This experience would not only make us better artists but better people.

Hell, I was even getting a decent-looking tan for the first time in my life.

If the point (not that we should be talking about that) of coming here was to achieve my true potential, I was certainly on my way. Sure, there were some distractions. But these were good distractions. The animals, the food, Clorie. All good.

And there were times when we all seemed to share the same energy, intensely focused on our goals. Though I suppose this may have had something to do with the pills.

I should talk about the pills.

The mysterious blue wonderments first appeared in the Eat Shack on Burger Day, mixed in so casually we didn't even notice them at first.

As we walked along the buffet tables, salivating over the meat patties and assorted fixins, piling up our plates, Clorie pointed at a small bowl and said, "What the hell are those?"

We paused our drooling to examine the new arrival.

"Candy?"

"Mints?"

Agony leaned in for closer inspection.

"They look like...pills."

They did. But as with everything else, there were no labels. Aspirin? Ecstasy? It was anyone's guess.

The fact that they resembled pills must have been enough for Agony. Without another moment's hesitation, he thrust his hand into the bowl and popped a couple tablets into his mouth, quickly gulping them down.

Clorie's mouth was agape. "Agony!"

"Hey." He shrugged. "Get in the pit and try to love someone."

"Wait..." Her eyes shifted back and forth. "Did you just quote Kid Rock?"

Yes. He had. And it couldn't have been irony, because he was the only poet who didn't know what that was.

Anyway, our willing guinea pig did not begin to foam at the mouth or die. If anything, he now seemed much more energetic and enthusiastic compared to his usual drab self, talking a mile-a-minute about his latest poem. So the rest of us shrugged at each other and decided to join in. Everyone except for Tomas, who informed us he was "straightedge, bro." Apparently that was still a thing. Well, good for him.

As for the rest of us, we figured we were already in the middle of nowhere with a bunch of strangers. Why not continue throwing caution to the wind?

And really, what kind of mind-expanding retreat would this be if we didn't swallow some random unmarked pills? If they even were pills.

Whatever they were, they certainly gave us a jolt. We felt an instant surge of endorphins and energy, started dancing around and babbling excitedly right along with Agony.

Thus, the group quickly concluded that the pills were good. Necessary, even.

Hell, with those things in my system, I felt closer than ever to nearing the vicinity of the kernel of an idea. Potentially.

"Okay, that actually looks really fun," Tomas said, watching us. He grabbed a handful. "Fuck it."

I think we were all ready to stop questioning things so much. It was time to finally let loose, give ourselves over to the farm.

Sacrifice our health and our sanity, all in the name of art.

Though it was after this point that things started to become hazy. Like the image of Eve's dead body, thoughts of my life before the farm became an increasingly fuzzy memory. Assumed the memory loss was a short-term side effect from the pills. Seemed like an even trade, considering how they made me feel.

Why linger on such thoughts anyway? What would I even be going home to, when I finally left the farm?

Anyway. I wasn't exactly eager to get back to the rat race, waste my time away for some terrible company just so they could fire me.

Shaking the vile thought of full-time employment from my head, I resolved then and there that my only focus would be the there and then, i.e., the here and now (at the time).

(Note: There go those tenses again.)

The scenery, the sounds, the casual, weird almost-sex. These should be the only things occupying my mind. This was my life now.

I was learning to appreciate things—everything, in fact.

One morning I noticed a rainbow. And I just sat there, and stared at it. All those colors, putting on a spectacular show, seemingly just for me.

We live on a crazy, beautiful planet.

Our resident poet Agony frequently joined me in this new appreciation of things. In fact, after taking the pills that first time, he had one of his "ideas." He brought us outside where he led us in some kind of primal ritual to, as he called it, "become one with the land." Mostly it was a lot of writhing around on the ground and getting dirty. Not sure if it made us any closer to the earth, but it was an interesting bonding experience.

Eve had once done something similar. Though her idea of harmonious symbiosis with nature was smearing cow shit all over herself and shouting "I'm Cow Pie Girl!" At the time we thought for sure that this must have been performance art, but her only answer was to fling some of the shit at us.

Oh, that reminds me. We were all starting to stink.

There were pills and art supplies and food, but not a single change of clothes or toiletries of any kind. This didn't seem to affect Agony much, since his clothes were already deteriorating when he arrived at the farm. The rest of us managed best we could, rinsing our wears in the stream, drying them on trees.

Perhaps there were showers or brand-new wardrobes in an undiscovered shack. For now, we accepted that the farm did not consider hygiene a necessity for artists.

Maybe it was the pills effecting my brain, but I tried to look on the bright side. The stink was a good thing, I told myself, maybe even necessary. For the creative process.

The farm stunk, the animals stunk, we stunk.

We were all bonded together in stink.

(Note: Maybe don't mention the stinking so much.)

THIRTEEN

Then there was the day we did shrooms.

In the midst of some bad weed withdrawal Agony wandered off, as he was known to do, stumbled upon a patch of funky-looking mushrooms in a field. As with the blue pills, he wasted no time in yanking a couple of moldy spores from the earth and tossing them into his mouth. They must have been safe to eat as, once again, he did not die.

The pills were helping, sure. But the influence of hallucinogens in our quest for creativity made a certain kind of sense. Those beat poets seemed to do all right with them, anyway. So when Agony asked me to join him on his trip, I figured what the hell.

We ingested what I imagine was an average amount, sat on a hill. For a long time nothing happened.

"Are we enlightened yet?" I asked.

"Think we're getting there."

"…those things weren't really cow pies, were they?"

"Shh. Look."

A sheep was walking toward us. Or we imagined it walking toward us.

This sheep (or sheep vision) stopped right in front of us, made a noise. Before I knew what was happening (if it was happening) we were reaching out, rubbing our hands over its fur. Its eyes were wide, but it didn't move. Just stood there, letting us touch it.

Mostly we just sat there though, on that hill.

At one point Agony looked at me and asked, "Why don't you try experimental?"

"Huh?" I looked back at him. "Oh. I'm, like, open-minded. Tolerant, and all that. I mean, love is love. Whatever. Just not quite into it myself…"

"What?"

"Experiment?"

"Experimental? Writing?"

"Oh." I nodded, breathing an internal sigh of relief. "You mean, non-narrative?"

"Yeah, man. Could be cool."

This approach had not occurred to me.

Abstract would mean I wouldn't need a story. Wouldn't need to worry about structure, character progression. Shit, even grammar. Maybe Agony was on to something.

Probably still need an idea though…

We sat on that hill for a long time, Agony and I.

I won't pretend to remember the rest of our conversation word-for-word, but I'd venture to say it went something like this:

"When do they kick in?"

"Huh?"

"Yours kick in?"

"Kick in."

"Yeah."

"Heh."

"Heh."

"Think they kicked in."

"In."

"…"

"…"

"Yeah."

"Hmm."

"Do you miss your phone?"

"I'm still not sure."

"I don't."

"That's good."

"I don't want to be a part of the megadata."

"Yeah, man."

"My life is mine. It's supposed to be mine."

"You should write that down."

"The greatest minds of our times were allowed to just…think."

"Gets boring though. All that thinking."

"Yeah…"

"Yeahhh."

"I want to write an epic poem."

"Nice."

"The title just came to me: THE WEEPING BEAST."

"That's excellent."

"Thank you."

"You like poems."

"I've got something to say. And it's…something. And people need to hear it."

"Yeah. Open their minds."

"People conform."

"Don't know what else to do."

"You like to write."

"I've read a lot."

"Books."

"Bury me in my books."

"My life…is a poem. Poem. Pooohh-emmmm."

"…"

"In ancient times, scribes would write down the poems of their masters. Now the scribes are the masters of the poems."

"…"

"…"

"Remember when Eve killed that cow? That was pretty wild. Now she's dead…"

"That sheep was cool."

"Animals, man."

"Yeah. They're all right."

"We should look to the animals."

"Seek, and you shall know."

"The fuck?"

"Yeah, man…"

"Hmm."

"Like, think about it."

"Ha."

"It's all perspective."

"Hold on. Who's speaking right now?"

"I am."

"No."

"Yes."

"I've lost the narrative!"

"That's all right."

"Are we enlightened yet?"

"Think we're getting there."

"Good."

I stopped and listened to birds chirping, realized I had spoken that last line of dialogue. Now Agony was speaking again.

"Waking from a dream can be the loneliest feeling in the world."

"Damn. Spinning gold today. You should write that down too."

"Lost my pen."

"Are we sitting in poison ivy?"

"Maybe. Think Clorie will fuck me?"

"…"

"I mean, like…she said she wouldn't fuck us…but she might fuck me…"

"Ha."

"Heh."

"I don't know, man."

"I do miss some things. Toilet paper. Porn."

"Yeah. Porn was nice."

"I like when the girl treats the guy like shit. Steps on him, spits on him."

"Reminds me of high school."

"I think about that a lot…"

"Fucking."

"Yeah."

"Happens."

"Yeah."

"…think we should be thinking of ideas?"

"I ejaculate ideas!"

"Are we enlightened yet?"

After the comedown, I did some wandering of my own, went on a walk. Looking for a scarecrow.

See, there were rumors of a scarecrow on the farm, and I wanted to find it, look at it up close. Was hoping it would inspire something in me.

The scarecrow. The scarecrow holds all the answers.

Okay, this was an idea Agony and I had come up with while tripping. Still, I was getting desperate.

Time was ticking. I had to write something. Somehow.

Anyway, after walking for a while I got really excited because I thought I had spotted the scarecrow. Turns out, it was something I thought I had only imagined seeing before.

Another person.

At first I only saw the back of him. He wore dirt-smeared overalls and looked like he might be a farmhand, which, you know, made sense. Appeared hard at work, planting seeds into the dirt and raking.

So there are workers on the farm, I remember thinking. *Other people.*

These workers had certainly gone out of their way to make sure they didn't disturb us. Never saw or heard them, nor any heavy machinery. Must have prided themselves on working by hand.

The man stopped, used his sleeve to wipe the sweat from his brow. I was able to get a better look at him. He was an older gentleman with gray hair and leathery skin. There was a vacant, tranquil look on his wrinkled face. I wondered if this was the same person I had glimpsed through the window that night in the Eat Shack.

I moseyed closer in hopes of striking up a conversation, maybe even learning some information about this place.

"Hello." I held my hand up as I approached.

He lifted his head and squinted over at me, sweat glistening in the harsh sunlight.

"Sorry to bother you," I said, stopping a couple of feet away. Didn't want to startle him, make him run away. "Was hoping you might care to chat a bit."

He continued to squint at me.

Inching forward I said, "I'm a writer. Part of the new crop. Crop of artists, that is." Allowed myself a chuckle at my little joke.

The man nodded slowly before finally responding in a low scratchy voice.

"Yup."

I held out my hand. "Name's Art."

The old man considered it, eyeing my hand as if it were a varmint that had snuck into his garden. Promptly returned to raking the freshly planted dirt.

I lowered my hand. Bobbed on my heels, trying to be casual.

"Heard there was a scarecrow around here somewhere."

"Yep."

"You know where it is?"

"Yup."

"Okay."

"Yep."

"…and where would that be?"

"Yup."

The old coot was going to be a tougher nut to crack than I originally thought. That was okay. Had time to kill.

"Must be hard to do all the farm work manually."

"Yep." He nodded, still focused on raking the dirt.

"Unless you, uh…ya'll got silent tractors out here or something. Futuristic ones. Ha. I'm bustin' your chops. But seriously though. We haven't heard a dang peep out of anyone since we got here…" At some point during the conversation I had acquired a down-home, folksy accent. Guess I was trying to relate to the man so he would in turn impart wisdom to me. That's what these types of people did. Old farmers. Salt of the earth and all that.

"Yup."

"I suppose you guys know what you're doing though. Farm looks great, I must say. You've all done a hell of a job."

Should I bring up Eve? Perhaps it would be out of line for a guest to question such a thing. Better play it safe. Talk about myself.

"I tell ya, I got a nasty headache. Those blue pills are great and all, but you wouldn't happen to have any aspirin, would ya? Don't have my gout medicine with me, either. Weren't allowed to bring anything with us. Which is fine, by the way. Better that way, in fact. Anyway. Hopin' to avoid a flare-up. Horrible thing, gout. You got gout?"

"Yep."

The old man dropped the rake before turning and walking passed me.

"Then you know what I'm talking about." I squinted toward the dusk-lit valley. "The pain. I got it bad in my left foot. And all them fatty foods you guys feed us ain't helpin', let me tell ya!"

"Yup."

His voice was faint now as he continued to walk away, I assumed to get a new tool or something.

I continued a bit louder. "But yeah, this is some fine land ya'll got here. Do you own this farm or...I mean, not like it matters. Just curious. Curious about a few things, to be honest."

From behind me came the sound of a dull thud along with a sharp snap.

I turned around. A few yards away I saw the old man, a thick rope around his neck, his body swaying ever so slightly from side to side.

He had hung himself from a tree.

I was no expert, but the look on his swollen face seemed to suggest he was already dead, had likely died instantly by breaking his neck.

My legs began to move my body back in the direction of the Art Shack.

Upon entering I saw Clorie busy as usual, working on a new piece. Tomas was pacing back and forth, muttering to himself excitedly, about what I was unsure. Was only able to make out the occasional "bro."

I moved silently, not wanting to disrupt the creative process, worry the others with any more bizarre death nonsense.

"What's up, Art?" Clorie asked, luckily not looking up from her painting.

"Ah, not much." I sidestepped across the room to a shelf full of supplies. Grabbed the X-ACTO knife that Eve had once used to stab herself and kill a cow. Figured it must be pretty sharp.

"Are you going to work on your—"

"All right, see ya." I slipped through the door, slamming it shut behind me.

When I got back to the tree the farmhand's body was still hanging from it, confirming that this was not, in fact, some insanely vivid nightmare. Though I still held onto the hope it might be a residual hallucination from the shrooms.

I grabbed the nearest branch, hoisted myself up into the tree. Used the blade to saw the thick rope until there was a snap and the body fell to the ground, crumpling in on itself in a sickening fashion.

I held my breath and looked around. Satisfied that no one had heard, I jumped down. Lifted the old man's arms, dragged him along the ground, deeper into the woods.

Found a good spot. Covered the body in foliage and branches. Brushed my hands together, satisfied.

At least I accomplished something that day.

USE OF A LITERARY DEVICE
II

My wife and I were hosting a small dinner party.

The attendees were mainly acquaintances of mine whom I hadn't seen in some time. Most of them considered themselves artists. Now, like me, they had gotten older, didn't do anything. Recoiled into comfortable lives of blind subservience and domestic safety. Found jobs they could stomach, that paid adequately. Some of them had even started to have children, a concept so foreign to my current state of mind that it teetered on abstraction.

I was jobless, coming down from the euphoria of my spiritual (or whatever) awakening at the water fountain. My brain still buzzed with possibilities of the new life that lay before me, but it was starting to wane to a mild murmur. I wanted to keep the buzz going, to continue to feel excited, alive.

As Laura and I stood by the door waiting for guests to arrive, I tried once again to explain all of this to her. It was obvious my wife had little interest in my revelation, even being fairly dumbfounded by it. Being in a secure position at one of the top physical rehabilitation clinics—and actually enjoying what she did for a living—she could not understand the elation I felt at being free from my occupational constraints. I should be worried, panicking. She was certainly worried. Money, remember money? We need that, Laura would say. She was relieved at least for the temporary unemployment compensation while I had my head in the clouds.

Laura leaned over, sniffed me. "You forgot to put deodorant on, didn't you."

"What? No, I thought—" Sniff. "Damn it."

Then the guests were arriving, giving hugs, making kissy faces. Later, as we sat around the table, dining on chicken stuffed with some other animal, drinking bland overpriced wine, there was the usual chitchat. Boring stuff, really. So let's pick up towards the end of the meal.

The names and appearances of these dinner guests aren't important, by the way. Please use your imagination as to what they may have looked like. Maybe one of them had an eye-patch, or wore a funny hat.

Anyway, as I was busy ignoring everyone and sneaking Farley some scraps, the topic of my unemployment was broached. Like Laura, no one else at the table seemed to grasp that I was on the verge of a creative Renaissance.

"So you're just going to like, not…work?"

"Art never was the 'employed' type."

"Does this make Laura a sugar mama?"

Laughter. Wine sipping.

Obviously, they were jealous. I was going to pursue my dreams. Succeed where they had failed.

My mind was already starting to drift, to ignore the rest of the conversation, when one of the less sober attendees of this soirée began to babble about something that revived my attention. At first I thought I may have had too much to drink myself, as what she was saying made no sense. Something about a secluded gathering of artists. A "secret" retreat. She'd heard about it from an abstract painter friend of hers who lived in New York. She went on about how crazy all of it was between sips, a giddiness appearing on her reddened face.

"…a place where you can really get away from it all and be free to just *create*! Isn't that wild? And you're not allowed to bring anything with you. You're not even allowed to tell anyone where you're going! *You* don't even know!" And so on.

Needless to say, I was intrigued.

Apparently this painter friend of hers had been going through a period of severe un-inspiration. So he inquired for help from one of *his* friends who knew a guy, who knew a girl, who roomed with a gal, whose father's roommate's sister's cousin had once heard of a certain retreat. The painter became obsessed with finding out more about this secluded artist commune. Eventually, he was able to track down—of all things—a business card. A simple, cheap-looking business card, completely blank except for a phone number and two words on the back: "Become Inspired."

I thought the phrase sounded a bit hokey, not unlike a slogan for a new line of fashionable slacks. But like the painter, I found myself drawn to the idea just the same.

The thing is, merely learning of this retreat filled the painter's mind with all sorts of ideas. Something so unusual, so mysterious seemed to be enough to cure his creative block.

But he never forgot about the rumored retreat. Would spend evenings alone in the dark, sitting on the edge of his bed, just holding the card in his hand and staring at it.

It was quite the story. One so strange that there had to be some truth to it.

Ignoring the daggers from my wife's eyes, I prodded my friend with questions, increasingly excited about the prospects of such a creative haven. There wasn't much for my friend to tell, other than that it perhaps existed.

Another friend chimed in. "There is a certain…romantic notion to it."

"Yes," agreed another. "Like Thoreau, Ralph Waldo Emerson, off in the woods. Something like that."

Again, all of this was very exciting. Eventually, however, the conversation returned to the requisite reminiscing, gossip regarding mutual acquaintances. I sat there quietly, still fixated on the retreat.

Later, as everyone was putting on coats and making their exits, I pulled my friend aside. Asked (okay, whispered) if she would be okay with me reaching out to her artist friend. She thought for a moment, her eyes flickering back and forth.

"I just…want to ask him some questions. For research."

"Research?"

"Yeah."

"Research."

"For a book. A book I'm writing."

Art, what are you doing?
I had no idea and that only made it more exciting.
The feeling I had been searching for was back.
I was back in the park, at the fountain. Ready to dive in.

I awoke early the next morning, saw Laura off to work, took a walk around the block. Tried to clear my head. Came back home, attempted to busy myself with housework. Didn't work.

Sat at the computer. Clicked my inbox. There it was.
Grabbed my phone, dialed the number.
Felt like I was dreaming. My heart beat out of my chest.
The artist answered.
His voice was friendly, until I mentioned the retreat.
"No," was all he said at first.
"Um."
"Good bye."
"Really? I just need the phone number—"
There was silence on the other end, then:
"Walk away, man. Just forget about it."
My heart beat even faster. This felt dark, dangerous, like I was in a noir film or something.
"I'd like to look into it, is all—"
"Look. You got someone you care about?"
"Well, yeah…"
"Go to them. Focus on other things. Don't worry yourself with this."
"I'm not worried, I just think it would be…I don't know, cool, I guess."
"It won't be cool. No matter what you're thinking, that's not what it is. I've heard stories, man."
"…what kinds of stories?"
More silence.
"Hello?"
"Be safe."

Realizing he had hung up, I lowered the phone, stared at my face in the mirror.

Okay. I know what you're thinking.

This conversation, pretty ominous, right? A clear indication that I was in way over my head. Any rational person would take this stranger's advice, not pursue this risky endeavor any further.

The thing is, I wasn't feeling very rational.

I'm an artist.

Well, I would be. If I did this. Took the plunge.

I admit, I was stubborn, persistent. But maybe artists are supposed to be those things. The ones who make it, at least.

The retreat.

I had to go. It was my purpose, my fate.

Did I believe in fate?

Sure.

As long as I became a novelist, I'd believe in anything.

And hey, I did end up telling you this story.

Speaking of which.

FOURTEEN

The animals, the shrooms, the endless supply of pills and food. They kept us busy and content, that's for sure. But cracks were beginning to show—in some more than others.

Tomas hardly spoke anymore, mostly keeping to himself, only uttering the occasional "bro." He seemed lost, unsure of what to do without his little firecracker of an antagonist to bicker with.

Even though I was somewhat closer to Clorie than to anyone else on the farm, I still wasn't quite sure where her head was. Her moods, like her attitude toward me, seemed to fluctuate drastically. One moment she'd be laughing and the next she'd be staring off, frozen.

Agony was…Agony.

Leonard was mostly the same, though his old man rants grew even more cantankerous. One evening he really got into it. We were all sitting around the campfire as usual, having a normal conversation (well, for us) when he suddenly stood up and said, "How can we be here?"

The rest of the group glanced around at each other, unsure of how to respond or what this even meant.

Agony, who never had a problem opening his mouth and letting words spill out, broke the silence.

"Here is where we are."

Leonard shook his head. "We shouldn't be here. This was a mistake, can't you see? We're creating work in a vacuum. We have homes. Lives. I mean, what are we doing?"

"We're going home," Clorie said, "…at some point."

Leonard snorted. "Are we? How do we know that?" He looked around at us. "We've all thought about it, I know we have. The fact that we may be stuck here."

Again no one spoke. Leonard continued, "Even if we are going home, this whole thing just doesn't feel right. Artists shouldn't be secluded. Artists feed off of the world around them. Society needs us and we need society. It's cyclical. There's a symbiosis. Think about it. Right now back home, babies are being born. Wars being fought. And we're here in our little bubble. Away from the drama, the conflict."

Clorie shrugged. "Sounds fine to me. Who needs that shit? It's all just noise, distractions, bad energy. Besides, didn't you say yourself that we shouldn't be worrying about anything besides creating?"

Leonard sighed. "Now Clorie, don't get me wrong. This little excursion was fine when it was us and the elements, living off the land. It was all about creating, it was fun. But that didn't last very long. And now…" Leonard plopped down on a haystack, gesturing at our surroundings. "Things have certainly changed. I mean. Talk about distractions! We have this disgusting abundance of food, supplies…we're no better off than we were back home! And for shit's sake, what the hell kind of farm is this? What do they even grow here?" Leonard chortled and readjusted his glasses. "Not to mention one of us is just…gone. Poof. Vanished. I mean, come on. Somethin' ain't right."

Clorie thought for a moment, shrugged again. "You're probably…thinking about it too much. I've been guilty of that as well. I mean, how can you not be? Shit here is strange, and only getting stranger. But then I remind myself there's no point to anything." She gazed down at the ground. "We like to say things happen for a reason. But maybe that's humans trying to make the most of shitty situations."

"You can't mean that, Clorie." Leonard stared at her, shaking his head. "You were connected to things, back home. Fought for real world causes…political, ethical. You've told me about all the organizations you're a part of. You care."

Had Leonard and Clorie shared an intimate rendezvous that I was not aware of? I told myself he had probably cornered her, forced her into having a conversation with him. Yeah, that had to be it.

Clorie was still looking down, now etching in the dirt with a twig. "That still doesn't change the fact that the world sucks. I just do what I can to try and make it a little…less sucky, for some people. But I don't see it getting better anytime soon. Our president is a fucking joke, the economy is in the shitter, people are still needlessly starving and killing each other all over the world…hell, our country's on the verge of being involved in at least three separate World War IIIs…I mean—fuck it. I'd say we're about due for another ice age to come clear the slate. Start fresh." Her eyes flashed up at Leonard. "That optimistic enough for you?"

She was so dark. It was so hot.

"Yeah," I agreed, "why should we be so eager to get back home so we can suffer with all the other assholes?"

Leonard leaned forward with his hands on his knees. "Maybe the suffering is necessary to the whole thing! That's what I'm tryin' to say. The cycle of creativity, life itself."

"Maybe. Or maybe it just sucks."

He peered down his glasses at me. "There are good people back home too. What about that, Art. I mean. What about your wife?"

I folded my arms and leaned back on my rock. "Laura?" It felt weird to say her name. "Well, yeah…she's…"

"She's still there, in the struggle. Laura doesn't have the luxury of leaving the real world, all her responsibilities, going off to some fantasy camp. She has to work, right? Keep up with the house, the bills. Is that fair?"

I glared across the flames at that smug wrinkled face.

"You don't know fuck-all about me or my wife."

Everyone sat there awkwardly among the crackles and the crickets.

After a few moments I looked away, chuckling. "Besides, I'm sure she doesn't mind some time away from me too."

My little joke didn't do much to lighten the mood.

At some point in the silence Agony slowly tilted forward onto his head, pressing his palms flat on the ground. We watched as he raised his legs into the air so that they pointed straight up. It was actually quite impressive.

"If things get too much for you and you feel the whole world's against you," he said, "go stand on your head. If you can think of anything crazier to do, do it."

"That from one of your poems?" Clorie asked.

"I believe it was Voltaire," I said.

"Harpo Marx," said Agony.

"Ah. Close."

I was partial to the venerable sage Groucho myself. *"Whatever it is, I'm against it."* Was there ever a better philosophy?

FIFTEEN

The little thing—whatever it was—between Clorie and I became somewhat of an on-going thing. Our skin never actually made contact, so Clorie had essentially kept to her "no sex" vow from when she first arrived, but each time we were alone together was nonetheless intimate and erotic. For me, anyway.

We kept our dry humping a secret. The others didn't need to know, and it would only distract them. Besides, neither of us would be able to explain it if we tried.

Eve's death was likely the catalyst, providing the impulse to physically connect. A subconscious, primal urge to cling to each other, to the feeling of being alive. Even if the connection itself was as abstract as one of Clorie's paintings.

Or, of course, there was the other explanation: that Clorie had an actual attraction to me. Stranger things have happened, I suppose. Perhaps she found me complex? Viewed me as a sensitive young writer. Youngish.

Clorie and I did spend a lot of time alone together, sitting and talking. Much of this was done inside the farmhouse, on the couch we pretended didn't smell like a skunk had vomited while drowning in raw sewage. While eating rotten eggs. Did I mention it stunk?

Still, the original farmhouse was the coziest interior we had. Sure, there were no beds, blankets or pillows, and of course we had to piss and shit outside. But otherwise it was like our own little cottage.

Not long after the night of Leonard's campfire freak-out, Clorie and I were alone together on the couch for an afternoon nap. We awakened to a screeching cacophony from outside. This meant only one thing: Agony had found the bagpipes.

There were bagpipes, for some reason.

We had stopped questioning the logic of the farm by this point.

Anyway. Since we were now very much awake, Clorie and I began to have a one-on-one conversation—albeit one accompanied by a chaotic Celtic score.

She sat up, crinkling her nose, staring off out the window. She said, "I visited Eve's gravesite today."

I looked over at her. "How's the stick holding up?"

"Nice and straight."

"Nice."

I sat up beside her. Finally asked what had been on my mind for some time.

"Clorie. Uh. Is what we do, like…foreplay for you? For your art?"

Bagpipes.

"Yes," she said.

"I see."

"Nothing personal, Art. Right now I'd rather use the energy to create."

"Oh. Me too."

More bagpipes.

"Plus. I have a wife."

Probably waited too long to say that.

I changed the subject. Somehow started telling Clorie about the lone figure I'd seen out the window the night we discovered the Eat Shack.

"I think he was watching us," I said.

Clorie continued to stare for a bit.

"Probably."

"…you're not surprised?"

She shrugged. "Not really. This place has been one odd discovery after another."

"That is true."

"It's so fucked up and crazy here. None of it makes any sense. But it's all kind of…exhilarating, right? Never knowing what to expect. So instead of worrying, I try and focus on what I came here to do, use that energy to create."

"Along with…sexual energy."

"Right. I guess."

"Hmm."

I leaned in, started to blow on her shoulder.

"Not now." She turned away. "I'm all art-ed out today. Sorry Art. How about you though? How's your novel going?"

I straightened up, looked away. "Umm…it's been going…okay." Reached into my pocket for my pack of cigs, pulled one out and lit it. Puffed on it, surely looking very casual and cool.

Clorie scrunched her face, waving the fumes away.

"You smoke now?"

"Sure. Always meant to start. Mostly so I could take more breaks at my job."

"Right. So. Where are you?"

"Huh?"

"With your book."

"Like what page, chapter?"

"Sure."

"…does my smoking bother you?"

"Why should I care?"

You care, Clorie. I know you do.

"I'm just asking—"

"Art. Your book."

"Oh. I'm still in the outline phase."

"So you work with an outline."

"What. Is that bad?"

"No. Some authors do that. Others get an idea and start writing. See what develops. Sometimes even surprise themselves along the way."

I gave this some thought. "Yeah…I'm actually scrapping the outline. Going to do it that way now—the way you just described."

"Oh, okay. So you…do have an idea."

"Of course!" An odd-sounding laugh escaped. "An idea. Yes. Idea, yes I do."

"Okay."

"I, uh…don't like talking about it. Too early in the process, you know."

"Sounds like the opposite of Leonard. Can't get him to shut up about his ideas. Apparently his writing has been going great since he got here."

"Oh. Good for him." *What an absolute prick.*

"Have you tried using the typewriter in the Art Shack? Might help to change up your approach."

"Typewriter?" I'd noticed the dusty machine before but hadn't given it a second thought. "Yeah, maybe." I decided to change the topic again. "So, how long have you been at the whole…painting thing?"

"Like, in general? Since forever."

"That's dedication."

"Can't remember a time when I wasn't drawing or painting. Always been drawn to it. Ha. Was that a pun? I hate puns. Anyway. Yeah, since I was a wee girl. Can't seem to break the habit, I guess."

I nodded, blowing out smoke. Yeah, I probably looked pretty cool.

"Getting older though," she was saying. "People only want to see new things from the young and attractive. Young people inspire hope. Hope for the future. Once I hit thirty that was all over for me."

"Thirty's the new forty," I tried to convince both of us. "Thirty and flirty."

"Right…"

"Clorie, um. How do you do it?"

"Mm?"

"Make stuff."

She laughed, thinking I was joking.

"The pills help. That's for sure." She shook her head, looking at the floor. "Hard for me to focus, especially back at home. Too much shit going on in my life, my brain. And when I did start a new piece I'd take forever with it, agonize over every detail. Worry about what everyone would think. Here, I don't do that. I just…create. I don't waste time thinking about all of that shit. Can't do it to myself anymore. Now I just get it out of me as quick as I can."

"Like a fart."

"…y-yeah. I guess you might say that."

I took a good long drag on my cig.

Clorie looked up at me. "So, yeah. Now I create for myself. And I'm learning that makes me happy."

I nodded, exhaling smoke in an indifferent yet dramatic fashion.

She shrugged. "Who knows. When we get back home, maybe I'll even sell some of my paintings. I'm sure it won't be enough to live off, at least not at first, but…"

I nodded again, looking at her now, taking her in. "Yeah."

Clorie fidgeted on the springy cushion, sat on her hands. Maybe the smoke was bothering her. I put out my cigarette, stubbed it into the arm of the couch like some rebel who didn't give a fuck, had no cause whatsoever.

I may never be bohemian, but I could probably keep up this smoking thing. Well, until I die from it.

Clorie was gazing off into nothingness again. The bagpipes had finally stopped. It was just the two of us, there on that couch, on that farm, only the two of us in the whole world.

She said, "It's so weird that we're here."

"…me and you?"

"All of us. And we're all here for the same thing. Something we refuse to stop chasing because we believe it makes us who we are."

"Inspiration."

"Sure. That's part of it."

"Well, I'm always here if you need any…uh, inspiration."

"Right. Thanks, Art."

I gazed over at a corner of the room where the canvasses of Clorie originals were beginning to pile up. "It must feel great to finish things. Like giving birth, or something." I looked back at her. "Not because you're a woman. I, uh…would like to give birth too. If I could."

"Uh huh…"

"I'm a feminist."

"Okay."

I quickly lit another cig.

"Know how when you were younger," she said, "and you'd have a weird idea among a group of friends? Something you all planned to do or make together. Everyone would get excited about it in the moment, then forget about it. Well, I was the one who actually followed through, tried to make them a reality." Clorie shook her head. "To me these ideas were real, no matter how far-fetched or crazy they seemed to everyone else. To my friends, it was just a lark, a gag that never really meant anything. It was never that way to me. I'll die living the dream. Trying to live my dreams."

Wow. Okay. I wanted to say something here. Show her that I felt the same way, that she and I were essentially the same person. That we were meant for one another and that's why we were here. Fate. I believed in it, sure.

Laura.

What?

Laura.

An image popped into my head, a face, a woman. My wife. I felt a twinge in my chest.

The door of the farmhouse swung open.

Agony entered, acoustic guitar in hand.

"Yo."

I took another puff of my cigarette, nodded toward him. "No more bagpipes?"

"Nah. Not my style. But yo, check it out. I wrote a punk song. It's actually the same chord structure as a SOUND DUNGEON song, 'ENDLESS PIT OF DEMONS.' Hope no one notices."

"Think you're good."

He began to sloppily strum the same two ugly power chords over and over, as if in mockery of what a punk song was.

"*Nihilism,*" he sang, "*Nihilism…*"

Clorie and I listened politely. It was, at least, *passionate* nonsense.

After the full forty-five seconds, Agony lowered his guitar and looked at us.

"What'd ya think?"

"Punk as fuck," I said. And I kind of meant it.

Seemingly satisfied with this assessment, Agony turned and walked back out the door, leaving Clorie and I alone again.

"I'm gonna go hide those bagpipes. And anything else I find that can possibly emanate sound." Stood and stretched, stubbing out my death stick. "Maybe chat with Leonard too, see how his novel's going. Fuck with him a bit."

Clorie had already fallen back asleep. If there was a blanket, I would have covered her with it. I'm just that kind of guy.

SIXTEEN

Leonard's writing spot in the woods was a good walk from our main hub. As I wandered over I thought about what he'd said at the campfire, about how being isolated from the world might not be a good thing. Wondered what newsworthy events were taking place back home. What wars were being waged, which terrorists were blowing up whom. Quickly remembered I was better off not knowing.

Why the hell would Leonard want to be connected to all that shit? Why would anyone?

Leonard did his writing in a secluded clearing next to a peaceful, trickling stream. He usually lay on his back in the grass, bottoms of his jeans rolled up, hairy feet resting on a log, chewing straw. Real *Tom Sawyer* shit.

Emerging into the clearing, I found Leonard all right. But this time he was sitting on the log with his open notebook next to him, looking out over the water, his face covered in sweat. One hand held a pen and the other hand was down the front of his pants. He was grunting awkwardly and seemed to be in the middle of a particularly rousing inspiration session.

"Oh, okay," I said, instantly turning around.

"Fuck. Hey. Art. " I glimpsed back to see Leonard almost falling off his log trying to zip up.

"It's…uh, it's okay."

"Shit. Sorry." He was standing now, hands on his hips. "Sometimes I get…stuck. Need a little *stimulation,* so to speak. Bit of a release. Little dingle to my dangle."

I winced, still with my back to him. "I get it."

"…you're not going to tell anyone, are you?"

"Um. No. I plan on forgetting as soon as possible."

Leonard breathed a sigh of relief, wiped his glistening forehead.

Deciding it was safe to turn around, I made my way over to lean on a nearby tree, tried to quickly steer the conversation in a different direction.

"Getting a lot of work done? Uh, on your novel?"

"Oh, yeah." He cleared his throat and sat down on his log again. Grabbing his notebook, he turned toward me. "Came up with a new character name today: Johnny Fire!"

"Johnny Fire?"

"Johnny Fire."

"Nice."

"Leaps off the page, don't ya think?"

"Sure."

"Johnny Fire."

"Johnny Fire."

"Johnny's the newest recruit onboard Starship 5421, a vessel originating from the tyrannical planet of Tegh. You see, this particular volume picks up with our crew as they're traveling through the Nebyoona-12 star system en route to—"

Leonard was a hotbed of ideas, none of them good. Still, he seemed genuinely excited and even enthralled by his own stories, whether or not they had that effect on anyone else.

His ideas clearly turned him on, judging from the scene I had walked into. The sheer possibilities of his characters, his worlds seemed to fill the aging hipster with a childlike giddiness. I envied him in a way. Of course, I'd rather let one of the pigs shove a wet snout up my ass than tell him that.

Leonard was talking about Johnny Fire again.

"Johnny's a hero, but a nuanced one. In fact he has a rather complicated backstory, the details of which the public will never even see." Leonard grinned. "Well, at least not till I'm dead and all my personal notes and journals are released. For instance, Johnny's a renowned wolf dragon trainer, back on his home planet."

"'Excuse me?"

"Wolf dragon trainer."

"Right."

"Yeah. Wolf dragons. Ha! They're indigenous to his planet. As are sky fish."

"Excuse me?"

"Sky fish."

"Right."

"Ha!"

Leonard shook his head, stood up with a sigh. "Anyway. How 'bout you? How's the novel going?"

"Making progress. Nothing as exciting as wolf dragons or sky fish just yet."

Leonard tried to skip a stone across the surface of the stream. We watched it sink with a comical *plop*.

"Subjective narrator?"

"Huh?"

He turned to me. "In your book. Are you using a subjective narrator?"

I shrugged. "Maybe."

"Don't. The reader doesn't need the thoughts and opinions of the narrator on every page. You're not having a conversation. Get to the goddamn point!"

"I'm guessing you're not a Vonnegut fan? How about *Hitchhiker's Guide*?"

"Comedies—sure. But in serious fiction, all that stuff is extraneous."

Serious fiction. Man, that sounded heavy.

Is that what I want to write? Wouldn't comedy be easier? Wait, that's supposed to be harder.

"But isn't the narrator a character as well? I mean, isn't it impossible to write truly objectively?" It was fun throwing doubt into Leonard's strict view of authorship, taking the old head down a peg.

"No way. It's all about the *narrative!*"

Am I too much of a character in my own story?

Worse yet, am I unreliable?

I took a moment to remember some of our most enduring unreliable narrators. Patrick Bateman from *American Psycho*, Alex from *A Clockwork Orange*, Humbert Humbert from *Lolita*. And of course, Holden Caulfield, that grouchy loveable little scamp. At least he wasn't a phony.

We stood there, looking out over the water.

"I'm just trying to write one true sentence," I said.

"Hemingway." Leonard nodded. "Decent quote. But the man was shit."

"Hmm."

"Overrated, in my opinion. I could write a sentence that would make Hemingway choke on his French whore's coochie."

"He liked French whores, huh?"

"Yeah, he was into all that shit." Leonard sniffed loudly. "Real pervert."

"What a creep."

"You gotta look to your Ray Bradburys, your Asimovs, your K. Dicks...authors who thought outside the box. Really used their imaginations. Anyone can string some brief sentences together about a bunch of well-to-do windbags who talk too much, drink too much wine, hang out in cafes all day."

"He was sparse, though. Hemingway."

"Sparse." Leonard scoffed, folding his arms. "More like lazy, if ya ask me. There's no descriptors, not enough detail. Hell. I once wrote three pages of description for a coffee table."

"Must have been some coffee table."

"There was a lot on it."

"The coffee table."

"Right."

"I'd like to read about it someday."

We were possibly getting to the bottom of Leonard's ridiculous page counts.

He put his foot on the log, stretched his leg. "Hemingway did know how to describe weather, I'll give him that."

"Elmore Leonard said you should never describe the weather."

"Psh. Some of my best passages are about weather."

"Elmore Leonard also said you shouldn't describe your characters' appearances. That you should leave it to the reader's imagination."

"This Elmore guy sounds pretty lazy too."

I shrugged. "Sold a lot of books. He's dead now, though."

"Good!"

"Almost all of our literary heroes are dead."

"More room for us!"

"Gotta go," I said.

"Get an idea?"

"Gotta pee."

Night fell quickly.

Darkness swallowed the woods around me as I made my way back toward the farmhouse. The only sounds were crickets and the crunching of leaves beneath my feet. To keep from getting freaked, I tried to return my thoughts to ideas for my novel.

The scarecrow. Need to find that scarecrow. He'll show me the way.

Goddammit Art, this is your problem. Focus!

I caught a glimpse of something that stopped me in my tracks.

A dark figure in the distance, like I'd seen on the hill.

Only this one was moving. Quickly.

I watched the stranger tread deeper into the woods, disappear.

Decided to do what any inquisitive writer would.

I followed.

Creeping through the misty woods, heart racing, I stepped quietly around trees and hanging branches, trying to keep the shadowy figure in my sights.

I was on an adventure. In pursuit of an elusive phantom. Close to unraveling the mystery of this place, the Mystery of the Farm.

It's like a detective story. A taut thriller. Fuck Leonard. I'll write sparse as shit. Real short sentences.

Finally the figure stopped in front of a massive barn. Looked like a barn, anyway. It was certainly much larger than the other manmade structures we had seen on the farm. And unlike the others, there were no windows.

This must be where they keep the generator. Or where our secret handlers keep their seemingly endless supply of food and art materials.

I very much wanted to find out. So I eased onto my knees and toddled over to a large plant to duck behind it. Breathing heavily, I peeled back one of its palm-like fronds and peered at the figure standing in front of the double doors of the barn. He was an older man, dressed in dirt-stained overalls, flannel underneath. It was amazing how much he resembled the suicidal fellow I had met before. He looked like something out of a Norman Rockwell painting, the kind of farmer you would see standing with a pitchfork on a postcard from the fifties. Only instead of a pitchfork, this one carried a long sleek metallic instrument like nothing I had seen before.

Watching, I settled into my spot behind the plant, attempting to keep my breathing quiet. It was all very thrilling.

Felt something on me, glanced down at a colorful caterpillar crawling up my arm. Flicked it away. No time to observe the splendor of nature now.

The man's head turned, his small black eyes peering through the trees. Looking right in my direction.

As I readied the floodgates of my nervous puckering butthole to open, there was a noise I hadn't heard since before I arrived on the farm.

A phone ringing.

The annoying chirping tune echoed through the darkness, like a siren from another world.

The farmhand kept his eyes on the trees as he spat and reached into his overalls, pulled out a cell phone. He spoke into it in a gruff and impatient manner, though I couldn't quite make out what he was saying. The conversation only lasted about fifteen seconds before the phone was dropped back into his pocket.

The farmhand finally turned to face the entrance of the barn again. With a grunt he lifted an immense, medieval-looking bolt that ran across the wooden doors and pushed inwards.

Instead of an opening, there was another door, nothing like the first. It looked militaristic, almost futuristic. All shiny and steel gray, like the instrument he was carrying.

The man turned to a panel beside him, pressed some buttons on a keypad. There was a green light from the panel along with a loud beep, and the new door *whooshed* open like something out of *Star Trek*. The light from inside was blinding, a fluorescent sun in the night. I watched the farmhand step forward into the white.

Once my eyes adjusted, I saw that the interior matched the look of the strange device and futuristic door. Slick, sterile. And it was huge, like a warehouse. There were rows and rows of small compartments from one end of the structure to the other. In one of these was a middle-aged woman whom I had never seen before. She was sitting up on something resembling a hospital bed. In front of her was a canvas on an easel.

There were wires and tubes coming from the woman's body, connected to a large machine beside her. Electrodes were attached to the woman's temples. The machine was beeping, generating strange symbols on a screen. There appeared to be some sort of dark fluid traveling through the translucent tubes. My eyes followed them back to the woman. She looked frail, depleted, cheeks stained with tears.

She glanced through the doorway and our eyes met. Her face tightened, lips trembling, opening.

The door slammed shut.

USE OF A LITERARY DEVICE
III

Things will likely escalate from here. I'll make this one quick.

The scene: my therapist's office—after my recent firing, after the dinner party where I found out about the retreat.

My current state of mind: a black hole of depression. In other words, the usual.

I sat in my little chair. Dr. Joel sat across from me in his big chair, with his bushy beard straight out of a seventies medical documentary. He took long pauses before he spoke, stammered a lot when he did, and smiled a lot but never laughed. Alas, nary a chuckle was heard in response to any of my witty zingers or astute observations.

Granted, I wasn't finding much funny myself, stuck at home in a limbo of daytime TV and fruitless job postings, unemployed and uninterested. Only at the urging of Laura, who at this point was genuinely concerned for my well-being, did I begin to seek help. This included seeing a psychiatrist, which led to being prescribed medication for my anxiety. Turns out I was anxious, to what they called an almost debilitating degree.

So here I was. Staring into the eyes of a man whose job it was to stare back, occasionally nod. Still, I had a pretty good feeling I was the doctor's favorite, most complex case. Surely he relished the opportunity to crack me open, solve me like a riddle. I imagined he stayed up nights pondering his new patient, all of his interesting, thought-provoking problems.

This may have been one of the reasons I was there in the first place.

"So, Art. How have you been?"

After breaking down in tears, regaining my composure and accepting a tissue, I said, "Good, and you?"

Dr. Joel's eyebrows arched halfway up his forehead. "Uh, good. Right. Where did we leave off last time? Ah, yes. You were telling me about your parents—"

"Fought a lot. Next."

"Um. Your childhood?"

"Lonely, uneventful. Read a lot, watched TV. What else ya got?"

Dr. Joel nodded slowly, sucked in his lips. He looked like a fish when he did this. I've always enjoyed fish, had a couple when I was a kid. Had I mentioned this to him? Perhaps he was subtly evoking these fish memories to get me to divulge the secrets of my inner psyche. If so, he had really earned that P.H.D. on the wall.

Either way, his silence got to me.

"Shit. I don't know." I was looking up, focusing on a tiny mark on the ceiling, hoping the tears did not return. "Life for me is nothing but a fruitless pursuit of the unattainable. I try to look on the bright side, sure. The world seems full of possibilities. Until I get out of bed. Then it's all downhill."

He scribbled something in his notepad.

"Why can't I be like everyone else, you know? Most people, they don't do shit. Live day to day. Wake up, go to work, come home. Do it again and again until they keel over from a heart attack or get hit by a bus. That's what I should do from now on. Give in. Become one of the herd. Enjoy a blissful, mindless existence until it's over." My gaze had drifted to the window behind Dr. Joel's head. There was a tiny bird out there, hopping on the ledge, peeking in on us. Why were birds always mocking me? "If I'm being truly honest, there's no point to anything and I should just give up."

Dr. Joel was nodding. "Are you feeling…suicidal?"

"…I have thoughts."

"…about suicide?"

"Well, don't go pressing any big red buttons or anything. Nothing that serious."

"I see."

"They're more like…temporary hallucinations. Driving off a bridge or a cliff or something. Romantic notions, really. I'm afraid of heights."

"Hmm." Scrawling again in his notepad.

"Don't worry. I could never do it, commit suicide. Even the word *commit*, jeez. Bit too final. Though there is a certain passion to it." I shrugged. "Anyway. Figure I might as well stick around. See how the shit-show turns out."

Scribble, scribble. "Are you taking your anti-anxiety meds?"

"Started them."

"How does that make you feel?"

"Anxious."

Is this a vaudeville routine?

"Okay…" he said. "Tell me more."

"I'm restless."

"Restless."

"Right. Like I want to do something, but I don't know what." I shrugged again. "Probably for the best. Like I said, doing stuff is hard."

"Something. Like, make something?"

"Sure."

Dr. Joel nodded a long time before he spoke again. "Giving of yourself, putting yourself out there in the world, is indeed difficult. And it is true that there are both doers and non-doers. But something in my gut tells me that you are ambitious, Art. That you want to be a doer."

I looked back at the window. The bird was gone.

"Yeah. I want to make something. Something creative, original. That only I could make."

Dr. Joel crossed a leg, folded his hands in his lap. "Creativity takes time. Some take more time than others." When I didn't say anything, he continued. "It's okay to question things, Art. To get sad sometimes."

"I get real sad."

"Your medication should help with that, once it kicks in."

"Good. I'll keep my head out of the oven for a little longer."

"So…to clarify…you're *not* suicidal?"

"Nah. Heh. Probably screw it up anyway. Be better off hiring a hitman to do the job."

Dr. Joel slapped his knee, leaned forward. "Now that's creative! See, you have a very active imagination, Art. You have ideas."

"Mostly dark ones."

"That's okay!"

"Weird dreams, too."

"Ah, yes. The reoccurring one?"

"Where it's the last day of high school? I'm wandering around an empty building? Yeah."

"We've discussed that a bit."

"That day was supposed to be something. Something memorable. But it wasn't, at all. Can't remember a single thing about it."

"So your brain returns to it, creates alternate versions."

"Right."

"That day was the ending of something…"

"It was supposed to be the beginning."

Dr. Joel leaned back in his chair, jotting more notes. Looked up again.

"What about the novel?"

"Hmm?"

"You mentioned before that you want to write a novel. That's exciting."

Another shrug. "What's the point? No one's going to read it. People can just watch a police procedural on TV instead. A show about doctors, maybe."

"You would enjoy writing it. It would mean something to you, no?"

"Hm. Maybe. But I should forget writing, forget about everything. Go live in the woods."

"Into the wild."

"Right. Like the guy, the book, the movie."

"Mm."

As I watched Dr. Joel scribble notes I noticed myself breathing. Was I having another panic attack?

He glanced up at me again, stroking his beard like a big bushy cat.

"Art. What is it that you want?"

I let out a childish groan. "Damn it. It sounds fucking cheesy when I say it out loud. I don't know. I want to write the goddamned great American novel, or whatever."

"Well, then. Do it."

"Do it."

"Write it."

"Right."

"Art. Let me tell you something." Dr. Joel placed his hands on his knees, leaned forward in his chair, suddenly with an expression on his face like an excited child. "I love hiking."

"...okay."

"Don't know what I'd do without it. Hiking is my life."

And here I thought Dr. Joel's every waking moment revolved around me.

"Last weekend I went to the Catskills," he continued, a big smile spreading over his beard.

"Cool," I said.

"The thing is, I used to be scared of hiking! I was scared because I'd never done it. Until I did." Dr. Joel whacked his notepad and shook it, the pages fluttering loudly. "You can do the same thing! That power is within you. To live the life you've always wanted, to write. This is your book, your story. You can change the narrative."

"*Change the narrative.*"

"Yes! All you need to do is take the first step. For that, maybe you need to...how do I put this? Get out of your own headspace. Leave your comfort zone."

"Well, *that* doesn't sound good for my anxiety."

Dr. Joel glanced up at the clock on the wall. "Ah," he said, "appears our time is up."

Slowly I got to my feet, felt the tears coming back. When was the last time I had cried before that day? Fifth grade? Someone called me a butthead or something? Now I was blubbering like a baby.

"I have to pee," I said.

Dr. Joel put his finger to his lips. "Interesting."

"Huh?"

"Oh, nothing. Just noticed that you, uh…always seem to have to urinate, when things become…too much."

"That's…weird."

"…yes."

Dr. Joel stood up, cleared his throat. I thought he was going to shake my hand, but instead he bent to open a small filing cabinet, began to leaf through it. I stood there, wobbly, biting my lip. Wanted to jump on him, cling to him, hug that big beard right off of him.

He stood again and turned to me, held out what looked like a small business card. He gestured with his eyes for me to take it. I did, slowly.

A phone number on the front. That was it.

Turned the card over. Two words in bold letters:

BECOME INSPIRED.

Dr. Joel cleared his throat. "I don't…uh, normally do this. Never…have done this, actually." I looked up at him. "But I believe you're a, uh, special case."

Knew he thought I was special.

"I can't vouch for it personally. But from what I've heard it certainly sounds…effective."

I looked down at the card again. Back up at him.

"A first step," he said. "The most important one."

He smiled gently, nodded.

"Good luck, Art."

And this, Dear reader, is about where you came in.

SEVENTEEN

"Is there something you want to talk about?"

Clorie was standing in front of her latest creation, dripping brush in hand. We were the only ones present in the Art Shack (mentally, anyway—Tomas was pacing, making faces in the monitor of his camera).

I was at my desk, trying out the typewriter like Clorie had suggested.

Now, instead of staring at a pad of paper, I stared at a typewriter.

How long can writer's block last? This is starting to get ridiculous.

Only thing I could think to type was "All work and no play make Art a dull boy." And that probably wouldn't end well.

Rain drummed lazily on the roof of the shack. Made me think of rainy days as a kid, watching *The Wizard of Oz* on TV, writing stories with my Gammy in her kitchen as she boiled eggs and drank Diet Cokes.

Nostalgia. Comfort.

What the hell did I write about back then? Gnomes or fairies or some shit?

Couldn't write now, that was for sure. Not with everything I had seen the night before still on my mind. The farmhand carrying that strange metallic instrument. The huge barn housing ominous machines and frail-looking humans. That woman's face.

"Art."

I realized that Clorie had turned from her canvas, with a look that indicated she was likely concerned about my brain.

She tilted her head and asked, "Would you like me to be your therapist?"

Did Clorie somehow know I'd been reminiscing of my sessions with Dr. Joel? Was she clairvoyant?

See Art, ideas are all around you. Stephen King got like eight stories out of telepathy. At least.

"Art?"

Shit. I still wasn't responding.

"Would you like me to be your therapist?" she repeated.

"…yes."

"Okay. I'm not getting anywhere with this right now anyway."

Clorie moved away from her painting with a sigh, pulled a wooden chair to the desk to sit across from me.

"What's going on?" she asked.

I took a deep breath. My eyes glanced around, doing a quick survey of the room. Tomas was still pointing a camera at his face. Agony was off either working on a haiku or riding a pig. Leonard was at his usual writing spot by the stream. Jerking it, no doubt.

"It's just…" I looked back at Clorie. "Think there's really a scarecrow?"

"Huh?"

"Can't focus."

"I can tell. Even with the pills?"

"It's bad. I know."

"What's on your mind?"

"Well. Right now…I'm wondering if Tomas is going to pop that pimple on the side of his face or if I'm going to have to do it for him. He keeps zooming in on it. It's gross."

"Umm." Clorie shifted in her chair. "I thought you were maybe…like, upset about Eve or something…"

"Eve? Oh. Right, Eve. That's definitely another thing that I am currently thinking about, as well."

Clorie's eyes told me how she felt without saying it—*maybe this guy isn't the sensitive artist I was originally drawn to.*

She was drawn to me, wasn't she?

"Clorie, I—"

Her eyes flashed at me.

"I...I saw something."

"Yeah. You told me. You thought you saw someone standing on a hill."

"No," I said. "Something else."

"We need to get our hands on one of those phones."

This was the conclusion Leonard came to after Clorie prodded me to tell everyone else what I had told her—about the warehouse and the tubes with the dark liquid.

We were all together now inside the Art Shack. Outside, the drizzle had become a downpour. Wind howled, rattling the shutters.

As I relayed the story to them, the group stood staring at me, mouths open. I had never seen them all so simultaneously enthralled. Even after I was finished, my mouth kept going. It all spilled out of me. The first figure I had seen, the one standing on the hill watching us. The farmhand I met later on—the one who hung himself. Remember that guy?

This last tidbit caused a bit of a stir.

Once the yelling and cursing quieted down, Leonard shook his head and peered over his glasses at me. "All right, we need to think here. Art, you're an idiot for not telling us sooner. But we'll deal with that later. Right now we need a plan." He stroked his whiskered chin. "If this farmhand you saw was using a cell phone, that means they have reception. And that means we can call for help."

The responses from the group came at once:

"We would need a phone first."

"This is crazy."

"Are you sure it wasn't a walkie-talkie?"

I responded to the last one. "Walkie-talkies don't ring. Anyway, that's what I saw. Thought I saw, anyway. It was pretty dark."

Agony had been staring at the floor during all of this. Finally he looked up and glanced around at us, scratching the back of his knotted head. "Um...hate to be, like, contrarian here—not a 'team player' or whatever. But maybe we should hold off on doing anything. At least for the moment. Been getting a lot done here. Even made progress on THE WEEPING BEAST." Ah, yes. The epic poem. "So how 'bout we just, like...chill for a bit?"

The others stared at him, dumbfounded. Agony went to scratch his cheek, and I noticed for the first time that he had a nasty cut on the back of his hand.

"Pig bit me," he said when he saw me looking. "Actually. Do we have any, like...medicine?"

Sidestepping this less pressing matter, Leonard sighed and said, "Agony, I understand you're being productive. Hell, I've been writing up a storm lately. But let's face facts." He looked around, shaking his head. "All of this shady shit only confirms my suspicions. They've been keeping us fat and happy. Hidden from reality. Pumping us full of more drugs than Judy Garland!" He thought for a second. "Eve. She must have stumbled upon their plan...discovered something she wasn't supposed to. Like Art did. Only Art got away lucky. For now."

"What about that other dude?" Tomas was sweating, eyes darting back and forth. "The one who hung himself. What was that all about?"

Leonard was scratching his chin again. "Sounds like the guy was scared. Of what? Who knows. We'll need to investigate."

Clorie's eyes narrowed at him. "You're loving this, aren't you?"

"Huh? Clorie, I—"

"This isn't one of your fucking novels."

Leonard put his hands on his hips. "Well. There sure is something going on...maybe you can tell us what it is, Clorie?"

I cleared my throat. "We don't exactly *know* anything, really."

"Art." Leonard's beady eyes were on me again. "We've ignored the facts too long as it is. Assuming what you're telling us is the truth." He glanced around at the others, smirking. "Writers tend to have vivid imaginations." He looked back at me. "You sure you haven't been eating them mushrooms out in the field with Agony?"

Tomas cleared his throat before speaking again. "This barn or warehouse or whatever. What you say was in there?"

I shook my head, turning to him. "Weird machines. Tubes, man. Filled with dark liquid."

Leonard snorted. "Now that sounds like sci-fi!"

"Who was this...this woman you saw?" Clorie asked.

"She had a paintbrush in her hand and a canvas in front of her. So I'm assuming another artist. Think she was restrained, trapped. Being forced to paint."

Clorie looked away. The rest of the group stared vacantly.

Sighing heavily, Leonard stepped toward me. "How about this? We split the difference, so everyone's happy. Give it another day or so, play it cool...see if anyone ends up coming for you..."

I was beginning to think Leonard had ulterior motives. Wanted me gone in the hopes of being the only surviving author of this ordeal—the one to tell our story after it had become a global news sensation. He'd no doubt paint himself as the brave leader. A real badass hero, like Johnny Fire.

Or he just wanted Clorie all to himself.

Either way, the old codger was up to something.

"You mean wait till I get killed like Eve did?" I said. "That's what would happen, right?"

"...more or less. But hear me out. If they come after you, we'll know for sure we're on the right track. Maybe even be able to get the jump on them. If what you're telling us is true, of course."

I glared at him. "Easy, alien-boy."

Leonard held up his hands. "Whoa, whoa. All I'm saying is...we don't know *what* to believe." He smirked again at the others. "Like I said, us writers with our wild imaginations and all."

I felt a sudden flash of rage, tried to keep my cool. "You may want to rein in your own imagination a tad, Lenny...you've come up with a few stories yourself. And to be honest, this whole thing reeks of one of your ideas."

Leonard took another step toward me. "I would drop you so fast, son…"

"Try it, old man."

"You ageist bastard…"

Clorie stepped between us. "Boys, ease up."

Clenching my fist, I turned away. Noticed Tomas off to the side of the room. The others may have had their doubts about what I'd told them, but Tomas seemed visibly shaken. He stood there, shaking his head back and forth, muttering something over and over to himself. Sounded like "Don't want to die."

Decided to focus on him instead of Leonard. "Chill, man. Uh, bro. We still don't really know what's going on. And if we can find one of those phones—"

"No. This is bad, bro." His head stopped shaking, dark eyes peering into mine. "I kept thinking everything would be okay, even after Eve died. Told myself it was a fluke, that she did it to herself, or that she deserved whatever happened to her. Tried to be positive. Believe everything would work out if we kept our head in the game, kept creating. But, bro. This is bad. We're out in the middle of fucking nowhere."

"Give him a cigarette, Art." Agony said, glancing up from the festering wound he was picking.

"Shit." I patted my pockets. "Fresh out."

"Shut up," Clorie said. "You don't even really smoke."

"Freaking out." Tomas was muttering to himself again.

"Don't freak out, bro," I said.

"No, bro. I'm fuckin' freaked."

"Try to get…un-freaked."

"Can't. Too late."

Yep. Whatever was left of Tomas' brain had gone bye-bye.

Of course I understood why. The truth is, I was as scared as him. But the writer side of me was trying to view things from different angles, be creative. There was a solution here. We just needed to put our egos aside and work together.

Man. We were fucked.

Tomas slinked away until his back touched the corner of the room.

"Horror movie," he was saying. "This is a horror movie." Started shaking his head again. "The audience is yelling at us to leave, and we're not listening."

I could hear him breathing, see that his skin was turning red. Reminded me of one of my panic attacks. Only he wasn't paralyzed as much as ready to pop.

Then it happened.

Tomas screamed. Took off.

Shot out of the Art Shack and into the stinging cold rain. Sped across the dusk-lit field, still screaming.

We crowded the doorway, watching.

Tomas was making a run for it, leaving us all behind.

Maybe he'll make it, I thought. *Send back help.*

Our bodies flinched when we heard it. A sharp crack echoed through the valley, and instantly there was a misty spray of blood and brains where Tomas' head used to be.

Time slowed. Droplets of gore lingered in midair, mixing with the rain. A sickening confetti explosion of bright red across a landscape of browns and yellows.

The rest of Tomas slumped to the ground.

A man appeared, stepping out from a line of trees. He was walking toward us.

It was the same farmhand I had followed the night before.

Well. I was pretty sure.

Anyway. This time I recognized what he was holding. It was a very large rifle, pointed in our direction.

EIGHTEEN

"We're never going home, are we?"

Clorie said this to no one in particular as she stood staring at her canvas once again. I stood next to her, tilting my head to observe her most recent spattering of smears and blotches. To me they resembled Tomas' brains. Go figure.

This is the direction things are going. This is the story. I'm just the reporter.

This was Horror now. Sure. Genre would help people identify, label it. This was a good thing. All I had to do was add a couple jump-scares and call it a day.

The remaining four of us had been herded back into the shack by the man with the gun, the door promptly slammed shut. Based on what we had just seen we gathered it would not be in our best interest to make a run for it.

The rain had become more intense, beating down on our little Art Shack. Clorie continued to gaze at her painting, lost in her own world. Leonard paced back and forth. Agony sat in the corner of the room, scribbling in his notebook and babbling to himself. So, things were pretty much the same.

I moved to sit on the edge of my desk. Thought about death, about Eve.

Eve's demise had been mysterious, abstract. Up for interpretation. But Tomas. His death was much more…well, direct. Hell, we saw it happen. Not that this made the situation any clearer as to what was actually going on.

Leonard crept to one of the windows, peeked out into the darkness that had fallen.

(Note: Literally and metaphorically. Nice.)

His breath fogged the glass as he whispered, "What the fuck is this place?"

A grave stillness set in before Clorie's voice emerged again, not answering the question but posing a new one.

"Do you even remember your life anymore? What it was like?"

She turned to me. "Tell me something," she said. "Tell me about your life. I don't know anything about you."

"Tell you something. Like…anything?"

"Yes."

I thought for a moment, glancing at the others. Stood up straight and looked her in the eyes. Let out a heavy sigh, wet my lips. It was time I came clean.

"I…I get gout."

Dramatic pause to let this revelation sink in.

"Never told anyone that before."

We were nearing the end, figured my character could use an endearing emotional moment. Of course, it wasn't true. Not the gout, the fact that I never told anyone. My wife knew. And that farmhand I met for a couple of minutes. Though he hung himself after, so that didn't really count. Anyway, it was close enough to the truth.

"It really hurts."

Clorie scrunched her face. "Like—on your foot?"

Still peering out the window, Leonard nodded. "Gout. Mostly effects lazy, unhealthy people."

"Hey," I said. "I'm at least not one of those things."

"The King's Disease, they call it. Reminds me." Leonard turned from the window. "I came up with a new character today. King Jeron."

"King Jeron."

"Yeah."

"Is he a King?"

"Well, in a way. You see, on his home planet—"

"Enough!"

I'd never heard Clorie's voice so loud and forceful before. We all looked over at her. She stared back through thin strands of dark hair that had come loose and hung down over her face.

"Why did I come here?" she said. "What the fuck was I thinking."

I stepped toward her. "Clorie—"

"The government," Leonard said. His back was to us as he peered out the window. "They lured us here. The question is: why?" Leonard tapped his chin.

Clorie shook her head. "What?"

Leonard turned from the window. "The government. Buncha shady fucks, right? Maybe, just maybe—now hear me out—this farm is the center hub for a vast conspiracy *against* artists. They want to harness all the ideas and energy created here, use it to their advantage. To power massive artillery, aid in military strategies, wage war. Do what they do best: lie and kill lots of people."

"Right on!" Agony floated over from his corner, seemingly riled up by Leonard's current diatribe.

"Or!" Leonard raised a finger. "This place really is a farm. Only instead of crops or livestock, they farm artists. Harness our creative juices. Our essence…es. Ship it out all over the world. To generic home décor centers and department stores. Profit from our blood, sweat and tears. Literally! Think about it. The tubes, the constraints." Leonard's eyes were wide, crazed. "The government wants to milk us!"

"Yeah!" Agony shot his fist into the air.

"That's stupid," Clorie said at the same time.

"Art for the masses!" Leonard was now yelling above the sound of the rain. "The system wants to control art, make it into a commodity. Just like everything else. Fucking damn it all."

I was pretty used to Leonard's rants by this point, but this particular one had gone on long enough. It was outlandish. It was absurd. It was threatening to take over an entirely new page if I didn't step in.

"This isn't a dystopian sci-fi story."

"No." He turned, peering at me over his glasses. "It's real."

It is normal to want to search for answers when you have no clue what the fuck is going on. And even though Leonard was veering into some dangerously genre-like territory, it was clear that things had certainly taken a turn.

The weird thing was, the dire situation we found ourselves in was doing something to me. I felt like the gears were finally beginning to turn, my writer's block on the verge of being magically lifted. *And let's face it*, I remember thinking, *the more dramatic the events, the better the chance my book will sell. Not that I care about that sort of thing of course.*

Anyway, since we were throwing around crazy ideas, I decided to voice a thought that had been floating around in my head for some time.

Squinting around at the group I said, "I'm not entirely convinced you're not all simply physical manifestations of my own id. Different parts of my personality, or something."

Leonard sighed. "Come on, man. You can come up with something better than that." He looked at the others. "Art must have read *Fight Club*."

"Good movie," Agony nodded. "Right on."

Clorie laughed and I felt myself die inside a bit. "Yeah, or maybe he just saw *The Sixth Sense*," she said.

"What? No. I'm not saying you're all *dead*."

"Yeah." Leonard scratched his chin. "That reference doesn't track."

"Sometimes I feel like a ghost," said Agony.

I sighed and decided to drop this stale, gimmicky plot device—for fear of copyright infringement, if nothing else. Still, we needed something big and important for the third act. Answers would be nice. A revelation. Something to bring everything together.

Where was a good *deus ex machina* when you needed one?

"Anyway," I said. "Agony was on to something. We should keep working. Stay the course, concentrate on our projects."

"Art." The look on Clorie's face was not unlike pity for a babbling mental patient. "Our plan, remember? We need to steal a phone. Call for help."

I shook my head. "It's too dangerous. Safest thing would be to lay low. Wait for people back home to alert the authorities, come looking for us. Then I can show them the body, explain what happened."

Clorie's eyes widened. "What."

"Huh?"

"Body. You said 'body.'"

"Yeah. The body."

"What body."

"The body of the...you know, the farm worker guy. I told you. The one who hung himself."

Leonard stepped beside her. "You didn't tell us anything about a body."

"What did you do?" Clorie looked like she was about to vomit.

"I...well, I got rid it."

"The body."

"Yes."

"You buried the body."

"Sort of."

"Why did you do that."

Leonard clapped his hands. "This is great!" He looked around at us. "I mean. It's fucked up. But if we can find the grave, dig this guy up, there's a chance he might have a cell phone on him."

"Wait," Clorie said, looking back at me. "Eve. Did you take her body away too?"

"What? No, of course not."

Agony was picking at his wound as he asked, "So, like. Do you remember where the dead farm dude is?"

Of course I did. Hadn't even properly buried the guy. Just covered him with leaves and called it a day. The spot would have been incredibly easy to find. But for some reason I said, "I...I'm not sure."

"Art." Leonard peered over at me. "This is our only chance. Unless there's some magical jeep that's going to appear out of nowhere and help us escape. We need you to tell us where he is."

A magical jeep would make a great *deus ex machina*.

Taking a step back I said, "Guys, I'm serious. Let's just…see how things play out. Wait for people to come."

Clorie screamed, came toward me. "What the *fuck* are you talking about? *No one knows we're here*. No one knows where *here* is!" She shook her head, staring at me in disbelief. "You're sick. You actually…oh no. Please don't tell me you're using all this as…as *material*."

"Material?"

"For this magnificent best-selling paperback you're going to write one day."

"Of course not!" I would obviously print in hardcover first.

Leonard stepped to me as well, pointing a bony finger in my face. "If you think you're writing about this when we get out of here, no way. This one's mine. Has Leonard Stantz written all over it!"

Knew it.

"Oh, so you want to turn this whole thing into a generic genre piece." I rolled my eyes, scratched my chin in mock-contemplation. "Hmm. Aliens milking creativity from artists. Guess that's one way to go."

"Wait," Clorie said, slapping her hand into her face. "What are we even arguing about here? Book ideas? What the hell is going on?"

"And what would you do, Art? Oh, that's right. Nothing. You *have* no ideas." Leonard folded his arms, enjoying that one. "Face facts. You've never struggled for your art. Hell, you probably work for the damn farm!"

"Well now you're really being logical."

"Hey, at least I have an imagination! I'm the real deal. Not some hack wannabe, like you."

"Easy, Leonard," Clorie said, watching from the sidelines.

Too late. The gloves were off. Leonard had me on the ropes, was going in for the body blows.

(Note: Boxing references, too many or not enough?)

"You think you're like us, Art. That you belong here. Ha! Since I've known you, all you've proven yourself to be is a lazy, delusional asshole passing himself off as an artist."

Clorie stepped forward. "Leonard, please. This isn't helping."

He turned to her. "No, Clorie. Think it's time we all came clean about this little delusion of his. See, Art doesn't understand. We've dedicated our lives to our passion. Sacrificed everything to come here." Leonard rounded to face me. "What sacrifices have you made, Art? What hardships have you endured?"

Clearly Leonard had never experienced the pain of gout.

"Huh? Leonard, what does that have to do with—"

"Come on. What struggles have you ever had in your life, you…you straight white male!"

"Wait." I thought for a second. "I mean, aren't you—"

"I'm not straight!" He reeled back, seemed to ponder on this himself. "At least…not in the pejorative sense. There was this one time, see, back in my college days…"

"Guys." Clorie stepped between us. "Put the bullshit aside. If we ever want to figure out what the hell is going on or make it out of here, we need to work together."

She put her hand out in front of her, looked up at Leonard.

"I'm in. Let's do your plan. Find the body, hopefully find a phone." She glanced at Agony and I, her hand hovering. "Leonard's right about one thing. We need to do *something*."

Agony stared at her. "Right on," he said, placing his hand on top of hers (luckily not the one currently oozing pus).

Leonard smiled at them before adding his own hand.

Damn. They weren't this enthusiastic when I tried to make a team huddle happen.

They stared at me, waiting.

"I caught Leonard masturbating," I said.

They didn't even flinch.

Shit.

Guess I was in.

NINETEEN

A rock-paper-scissors tournament was held (no leaf-flipping necessary this time), which resulted in Agony as the winner/loser. And just like that, our fate was sealed.

"I got this," he said.

Once I had given my best guess as to the general direction of the farmhand's body, the others were gung-ho to put the plan into action. It was agreed that only one of us should leave, as not to draw too much attention. I still preferred to err on the side of caution, wait things out. And now that Agony was to be our savior, our chances didn't exactly seem any more favorable than they had before.

I watched him now, scratching his festering wound.

"Are you sure?"

"Yeah, man. No problem."

The rest of us exchanged worried looks.

"Maybe…we should go best two out of three," Clorie said, glancing at Leonard and me.

"Really. I got this. Just gotta sneak out all quiet-like, use my stealth skills."

Now I was really worried. "Stealth skills?"

"You serious, Agony?" Leonard mirrored my expression, pushing his glasses back on his bony nose.

"Guys, seriously. I got this shit."

Agony seemed pretty sure of himself. He was facing his doom head-on at least. That made him something. A hero maybe. No, that was too much.

After all, that bite on his hand was clearly infected, past the point of no return. Even Agony must have realized how little time he had left. The discoloration stared back at us, bubbling.

Agony noticed us staring, quickly lowered his hand and cleared his throat. "One thing I gotta hip you all to, though. I practice non-violence. So if things get hairy out there, I'm going to be doing a lot of non-violent resisting. A lot of screaming."

Leonard smiled, stepped in for an encouraging pat on the back. "We'll keep an ear out for ya."

The confident look on Agony's face faded and he became quiet, his eyes searching ours. The weight of what he had agreed to do seemed to hit him now. He swallowed. "Tell the people back home what happened here. The world needs to know." There was a beat before he added, "Oh. And all the awesome poetry I wrote. Tell them about that too. Make sure to publish that shit."

We assured him we would definitely, most likely do this.

A heartwarming group hug followed. After we all stepped back, Agony sniffed and wiped his nose with the back of his hand.

"I wrote a poem," he said, pulling a piece of crumpled paper out of his faded jeans. "Like, ten minutes ago. While you were all talking and stuff. May I recite?"

The rest of us glanced at each other. Clorie nodded. "Sure."

Here we go, I thought. *Haven't we been through enough?*

Agony cleared his throat, held the wrinkled page out in front of him, recited:

> *far from me and mine*
> *you will see there;*
> *a single black rose that grew*
> *in that dark old age*
> *when we were afraid*
> *and all of the beauty around us*
> *dared and burned,*

taken for granted;
never will we be a part
of what we once were
or what we find

After finishing, he stared at the ground. Nodded, folded the paper and looked up at us again.

I glanced over at Clorie and Leonard. They were speechless, their eyes wet. I guess I understood why. This poem had certainly been an improvement over his previous work, though that wasn't exactly saying much.

Agony held out the paper to Clorie.

"Here, Clor…" he said, "you can, like…have this."

Slowly, Clorie took hold of the paper and held it to her chest. "Thank you," she said, smiling through the tears.

"Cool. Right on. Remember. Publish that shit. Oh. And tell SOUND DUNGEON they can suck it."

Agony moved toward the door before pausing, turning to face us. He looked like he was actually tearing up a bit now himself. I guess the angels were getting ready to weep, or whatever the fuck he was talking about before.

"I don't want to die," he said. "I've got so much more to create."

"No. Don't say that." Clorie was shaking her head. "You're going to make it."

I looked over at her, so scared, so beautiful. She looked like she actually cared. That was when I decided that perhaps I should offer my assurance to Agony as well.

"Hey," I said. "You're gonna be fine." As I went to put my hand on Agony's shoulder I caught a whiff of his stench. Had forgotten about the stench. Opted instead to give him an enthusiastic thumbs-up.

"You're gonna be…okay."

I've got so much more to create.
   Those were his last words.

Well, besides saying "shit" a bunch while stepping in some as he disappeared into the woods.

The point is, we never saw Agony again.

Upon his dramatic departure from the Art Shack, the remaining three paced, waited. Needing something else to focus our minds on, we even tried to get some work done. Or at least *appear* to be getting work done (they were watching, we assumed). But it was useless.

Luckily, I was used to being unproductive.

I sat at my desk, staring at the typewriter. Clorie wasn't even looking at her sketch anymore. Just sat on the floor, gently rocking back and forth. Leonard was once again at his post by the window, peering out into the dark.

"Agony's not coming back," he said finally. "They got to him."

I leaned back in my chair, stretching and yawning. "I'm sure he's fine."

Leonard tilted his head, eyeing me. "Is he, though?"

I noticed that Clorie was looking over at me now too. Her swaying slowed to a stop. This was it. She needed me to say something important, something reassuring. Something that made any of this make sense.

> **(Note: None of this makes sense. I'm so tired. Someone, please, if you're reading this, come find me, help me for the love of all that is good and decent please someone come and take me away from this nightmare I can't take it anymore I want to die.)**

"Where was I?"

Wait, I didn't say that.

Where was I?

Ah, yes. This is what I said at this moment in the story:

"I've gotta piss."

"Gotta...pisss..." Leonard intoned, returning his gaze to the window.

Clorie's eyes narrowed. "That's...your idea?"

A smirk emerging on his face, Leonard said, "Art's never had one of those, remember?"

Fuck him. His time is past. I'll be the one laughing in the end.

I stood and went to the door. As I reached for the knob, I heard Clorie's voice from behind me.

"Art. Wait."

I turned to face her. She held out an empty paint bucket.

"Use this," she said.

I took the bucket from her.

She sighed. "You're stupid and an asshole and everything…but I don't want you to be dead too. So. Don't go outside."

"You forgot 'handsome.'" I like a joke, a bit of a chuckle in times of stress. I'm a big goof when it's all said and done.

"I really hate you."

A love-hate thing. That was our thing now. It was cute.

Leonard groaned, turning from the window.

"I'm going out there," he said.

Clorie and I stared back at him.

He looked at her. "…aren't you going to…ask me to stay?"

Clorie shrugged. "Yeah, sure. I don't want anyone going out there…"

"Me, mostly," I said.

Leonard shot me a look before turning to Clorie. I noticed he was going into his 'hero' pose, standing straight and tall, hands on his hips. "Agony's in trouble," he said. "The bastards captured him, or worse." He held up his hand as if Clorie was about to interject. "Now Clorie, there's nothing you can say or do to make ol' Leonard stay. I've made up my mind. No more waiting around. I will find Agony and uncover what the hell is going on at this place."

Clorie threw up her hands. "Okay," she said.

"Did one of your deep, complex characters make a speech like that in one of your books?" I asked him. "Johnny Fire, maybe?"

Leonard squinted at me. "You never had any respect for me, Art. I've been nothing but a joke to you. You hate everything about me."

"…you have nice calves."

We all took a moment to glance down at his calves.

My statement had been sincere. I'd taken notice of Leonard's calves as he lay out by the stream with his pant-legs rolled up. They were really something.

In the midst of this silent admiration I excused myself, went to pee in the bucket in the corner of the room.

"Leonard," I heard Clorie say over the ringing of urine on tin, "you can't go. You have no idea what to expect out there."

"Clorie, I have to go. Someone has to. We have to stick to our plan."

This reminded me of Leonard's real plan. To write a novel using our experiences on the farm as inspiration. Hell, knowing him, he'd turn it into a series of books, make it a goddamn saga.

I would not allow the readers of the world to be subjected to the bland, mind-numbing drivel that I assumed he wrote. He'd ruin it, end up making it into some nonsensical allegory for imperialism or global warming or something.

The guy doesn't even like Hemingway!

He must be stopped.

Shit, I finished peeing like, a while ago.

I zipped up, cleared my throat loudly.

"After giving it some thought," I said, walking back, "Leonard's got this."

"He does?" said Clorie.

"I do?" said Leonard, at the same time.

"Sure. He's written countless adventures that hinged on one person—or alien or whatever—overcoming the odds, taking charge and saving the day." This had to at least be in the general ballpark of the schlock he wrote.

Leonard scratched his chin. "W-well, I—"

"Stories of fearless heroes, venturing into the unknown, armed only with their honor and their bravery. See, Leonard's already thought all this through from every possible angle. And he's been doing it for a long time. Years and years. Hell, probably before either of us was even born." *Had to slip in an age joke.*

"Well, gee, thanks Art, but I, uh—"

Turning to him, I continued to sling my bullshit. "I know we've had our differences but...Leonard—you're a stand-up guy when it's all said and done. Tuned to a different frequency, sure. But that's a good thing, especially now. Who *but* Leonard Stantz could handle something like this?"

Okay, I was laying it on thick.

Clorie didn't seem to buy it. "You're talking about writing, fiction. This is real life. Like, actually happening. Why should Leonard put his life on the line?"

"'Cause he's a stand-up guy!"

"What does that even mean?"

"Hey!" Now Leonard was getting into the spirit of my bullshit. "Art believes in me! And I think he…he might be right! I *am* the only one who can do this. Hell, my whole life's been leading up to it!"

Clorie shook her head. "What?"

"He said he *is* the only one—"

"Shut up, Art."

"I mean it, Clorie," said Leonard. "I got this!"

"That's the same thing Agony said!"

"No. It has to be me."

Leonard must have really been caught up in the fervor. Because the next thing he did was grab Clorie by the waist, pull her toward him, and in a most dramatic fashion plant a big wet one on her lips. I stood watching, mouth agape. It was like something off the cover of a pulp novel from a bygone era. In that brief moment Leonard really looked like a goddamn hero.

Okay, more like a creepy old perv.

"Get the fuck off of me," Clorie said, pushing him away.

"Leonard." I held out the largest paintbrush I could find. "Take this. For protection."

Leonard gazed down at it. Slowly his eyes met mine and he nodded solemnly, clutching the brush as if he were being handed Excalibur itself.

"Thank you, Art," he said. "I was a bit heated before, you know. What with everything going on. I'm sure you're, uh…you're gonna be a great writer. One day."

Yes, I thought. *I will.*

Leonard grabbed my hand, shook it vigorously.

I'd only been spewing hot air, of course. Trying to build Leonard up, get him to leave. But looking at him now I saw a different Leonard. One with youthful energy, a fiery glare in his eyes. He was a Viking, a warrior, venturing out to slay the dark wizard. Granted, this is more an allusion to *fantasy* than *sci-fi*, but you get the idea.

Clorie and I watched him turn and walk out into the darkness.
Good luck telling our story now, ya dumb loser jerk.

Clorie and I stood on opposite sides of the room, silent.

Outside the world had grown even more violent. There was the threatening rumble of thunder, raindrops the size of small meteors thudding our rickety roof. The storm had arrived. All our hard work (mostly Clorie's) on the verge of being washed away. Any second now our little shack would take flight, lifted up on the wind. Float off to Oz. *Nostalgia.*

I looked over at Clorie.

Say something. Remind her of our unbreakable bond, all the sexy times we shared.

There was a knock at the door. We screamed and leapt into the air accordingly.

Once our feet returned to the floor from our Scooby Doo moment, our eyes darted at each other from across the room.

Clorie spoke first, her voice a faint tremble.

"S-some one's at the door."

"Yeah. Guess we should…open it?"

"Art. I…don't think that's a good idea."

I considered this.

"The thing is," I said, "I really hate the sound of knocking."

"What?"

This was true—a little extra backstory about your narrator. Door knocking was no good for my anxiety. Invariably, on the other side of the door, was a person.

"So I'm just going to open it. I'm sure it will be fine."

As Clorie continually mouthed the word "no" while shaking her head, I tried my best to reassure her.

"Trust me on this." Actually, it was polite of the scary bad guys to knock. Eerily threatening, but polite. "Plus it might be Leonard or Agony, back to tell us the coast is clear. That they hijacked a jeep or something to take us out of here."

"A jeep?"

"Sure, why not."

I made a move.

"Art, what are you—"

There was another knock. Man, I really hated that sound.

Pulling open the door, Leonard stood before me in the pouring rain.

His eyes stared blankly through cracked glasses. The color had completely left his face. This was because he was dead.

I knew this mostly due to the large bullet hole in the middle of his forehead. Blood oozed from it, trickled down his face with the rain, dripped steadily on the floor.

"Holy shit fuck Christ!" Clorie screamed, backing against the wall.

Leonard's body slumped forward, thudding at my feet like an oversized hippie rag doll. I peered down at the open wound on the back of his head.

When I looked up again it was into the eyes of an old farmhand in bloodstained overalls. This farmhand was different from the one who had shot Tomas, I was pretty sure. Either way, there was a big shotgun in his hands and a Clint Eastwood sneer on his face.

Liquid black from what must have been chewing tobacco spilled onto the floor, somehow more revolting than the blood draining from Leonard's head hole. He took one hand off the gun to wipe his mouth, some residual gore smearing his face, all the while keeping his aim and his glazy cataracts on me.

I looked down at the barrel of the shotgun, then back up at the wrinkled face of the farmhand.

"Why are you killing off the different parts of my personality?" I asked.

"What?" he said.

USE OF A LITERARY DEVICE
IV

We have reached our final deviation. After this, it's on to the big satisfying climax.

So. I'd like to discuss my wife.

Laura.

Haven't spoken about her much. One reason for that may be—big reveal here—she is no longer my wife.

I know, I know. Pretty dishonest, pretty *unreliable* of your trusted narrator to pull such a trick. Though the divorce paperwork has yet to commence, so technically I wasn't lying.

Anyway. I should start with how we met.

I was fresh out of college. Had my fill of strangers at the local watering holes, wanted to see if there were some slightly less drunk strangers out there. Decided it was time to dip a toe into this strange thing called the Internet.

Browsing meetups for lonely sad sacks such as myself, I found one that described itself as a "soirée." This made it sound important, not pathetic.

This gathering of wayward souls was held in a cramped, stuffy apartment on the outskirts of the city. Immediately I decided that everyone there was smelly and dumb, that this was all a terrible idea.

So there I was in the corner, slurping down the rest of a drink that was more whiskey than ginger, ready to duck out and call it a night, when out of the corner of my eye I saw her. My future ex-wife. She was sitting at a sad little foldout table on the other side of the room. People crowded around her, but she wasn't looking at any of them. Seemed to be in a world of her own, singing softly to herself, as if in a trance. I liked that. Could even hear her from across the room. Her voice was atrocious, but she didn't seem to care. I liked that too.

"Twenty-twenty-twenty-four hours to go…I wanna be sedated…"

Her lips barely parted as she sang, eyes cast down, dreamily doodling on the cheap tablecloth in front of her. More than anything it was her indifference that intrigued me.

Her name was Laura. Is Laura. But you know that.

I didn't know it yet. By the time I mussed my thinning hair and got the nerve to walk up to her, she'd abandoned singing and drawing, had switched to a new activity: rather obviously stuffing drink coasters into her handbag.

"You're stealing coasters," I said.

"Yeah," she said, still not looking up.

"I love coasters."

"Coasters rule."

"Very underrated."

"For sure. Gotta use protection."

"Circles."

"Circles are bad."

"I also love The Ramones."

"Who?"

"Ha."

I noticed a coaster she had missed, handed it to her.

"This is a good one."

Now she looked up at me. "Hey, thanks."

I looked around. "Man, this is the pits."

"Ugh. The worst."

"Bunch of duds."

"Who let the animals out of the zoo?"

"No wonder they can't meet anyone."

"They're ugly, and they smell."

"They smell, and they're ugly."

"All around, zero stars."

"Zero stars, all around."

It was amazing how easy she was to talk to. We spent the next few minutes making fun of the other losers who showed up in voices that were probably way too loud.

She was weird, funny, and totally unique. Not bad to look at, either. Long dark hair, cute button nose. I know it's a cliché to talk about the eyes, but *the eyes*. When she looked at me, all the anxiety and the neuroses and the bad thoughts seemed to stop. Everything stopped.

There were flaws. She was a workaholic, for example. But I didn't know this yet and it wouldn't have mattered anyway.

We decided to continue our conversation at the bar next door, both of us yelling over the blaring drone of shitty rock music. Remember grinning stupidly, relishing every moment. After my post-college dating disasters, I'd finally met someone not only attractive but also with a brain, an actual personality. She even had goals.

Learned a lot about her in that bar, from things she said and didn't say. She'd recently graduated from college as well, was a night manager at a physical therapy center. Told me of her aspirations in the medical field, of going into public health. She downplayed all this of course, but I could tell she was a good person who genuinely enjoyed taking care of other human beings.

We talked for hours, on into the night. The date that never ended. Inseparable from that moment on.

Years of courtship followed. An apartment, a dog. Then there was the house and eventually marriage. It was love, as close to it as I'll ever get. It was bliss, and I didn't deserve it.

We shared something, a life. Something real.

Though in the end none of this love, this life we had built, no matter how true or amazing, could save us.

Likely, the main reason for this—and I only realize this now—is that I let her down.

I tended to feel the crushing weight of existence more than her, was more sensitive to it. Let it get to me, let it get so bad that even I didn't want to be around myself.

Laura had bad days like anyone else. But she didn't have time to ponder life's existential quandaries. She was always busy, always doing. As I mentioned, she became somewhat of a workaholic, though I suppose there are worse things to become.

After finally getting her Master's Degree, she landed a job at a local state department office. An entry-level position, but she quickly worked her way up the ladder. She liked the challenge, liked her job. Through her work she helped others, made a positive difference in peoples' lives.

I wanted to know what it felt like. To be satisfied, fulfilled.

I was never happy. Always wanting something more, something else.

Perhaps it's an artist's curse.

Maybe it's just me.

Going to switch styles, tenses now. Don't worry. I'm a professional.

Here's a scene:

Our home. Right before I turned thirty.

I'm sitting on my couch eating chips, staring down at my dog Farley.

Farley is sitting on the floor, staring back up at me.

"Woof."

That was me, not the dog.

INT. HOUSE – EVENING

Our hero, ART, has taken another sick day from work due to his increasing anxiety and depression. He sits on the couch in front of a muted TV showing some Bela Lugosi movie, stuffing his hand into a big bag of chips, staring down at his little dog. The dog stares back in anticipation of his next salty handout. The door opens and Art's wife, LAURA, enters. She is carrying items from her job. Papers, laptop bag. Bringing her work home with her again.

She walks past Art, straight into the kitchen.

LAURA: I thought about going grocery shopping on the way home from work, but then I didn't.

Art eats a chip. Laura steps out from the kitchen, eyeing the lump on the couch otherwise known as her husband.

LAURA: You're depressed.
ART: I'm turning thirty.
LAURA: You're depressed.
ART: What did I just say?
LAURA: Thirty and flirty. You're a still a young man.
ART: Dead man.
LAURA: Age is just a number.
ART: Who told you that?

Laura stares at Art.

ART: Really. Who told you that. I want to know.

Laura turns and goes back into the kitchen, messing with some things for dinner. Opening drawers. Clanging, banging.

LAURA: You were home all day.
ART: Yes?
LAURA: You could have made dinner.
ART: Could have, yes. But, you know.
LAURA: I'd hate to distract you from your work.
ART: I work plenty. Hell, I'm always busy.
LAURA: You spent the whole morning on the toilet.
ART: That's not true. I also made coffee.

Art's hand returns to the bag of potato chips on his lap. He eats some.

ART: How do you do it? Go to work every day?

LAURA: It's what we're supposed to do. What we're expected to do.
ART: We're expected to die. We'll get there if we work or we don't.
LAURA: True enough, my dear. But we need money. To live. Hence, work.
ART: I hate my job.
LAURA: You could look for a new job.
ART: I'm depressed. You said it yourself. Besides. Why?
LAURA: Money.
ART: You don't say.
LAURA: Money for food.
ART: I am hungry.

Laura opens a cabinet.

LAURA: Want pasta? That's easy.
ART: Melted.
LAURA: Huh?
ART: Yeah. Melt it.

Laura steps into the room and stares at him again, holding a box of pasta.

LAURA: Melt it?
ART: Yes.
LAURA: Melt the pasta.
ART: Why is that so hard to understand?

Laura looks at him for another beat. Turns and goes back into the kitchen.

ART: I want it melted. Throw in a block of mozzarella, melt that in. Cheesy melt. Would like my dinner melted, is all. Too much to ask? For a man. A man about to die.
LAURA: You're not about to die. Stop being so dramatic, Art. You have your whole life in front of you.

ART: Depressed.
LAURA: Ever think about seeing someone?
ART: Like a therapist?
LAURA: I've talked to professionals. It helps.
ART: Like…talk to them?
LAURA: It's not the most absurd notion.
ART: No, no. I'm a big boy. No time for self-help. Have to get things done. Be a real person. Productive member of society.
FARLEY: Woof!

Laura laughs.

ART: I'm serious.
LAURA: You seemed more serious about the melt. Besides, I was laughing at the dog.
ART: I am serious. The thing is, I'm depressed.
LAURA: Then find something you want to do. Who knows? Maybe you can even make some money. Help us eat, live.
ART: Living's wasted on the living.
LAURA: Sometimes you're so dumb.
ART: You knew that when you married me!
LAURA: No I didn't.
ART: That's a saying. Just a saying I like to say. All the time. You know that.
LAURA: No I don't.
ART: You knew that when you married me!

So that was a scene. Okay, here's another:

EXT. FAST FOOD PARKING LOT – NIGHT

Laura and Art are sitting in Art's car, parked outside a McYumYum's fast food establishment. They eat burgers and fries while contemplating life.

ART: What year is it?
LAURA: Sometimes I worry about your brain.
ART: What year do you think I'll die?

Laura eats a fry. Art slurps a soda through a straw.

ART: Are we all just counting down until we die?
LAURA: This is what you think about.
ART: What else is there?
LAURA: Hmm.

Laura takes a bite of her burger.

ART: Is death all we have?
LAURA: What about food?
ART: Ha.
LAURA: Maybe death is everything. The whole point.
ART: That sounds like a way to live.
LAURA: It's one way.
ART: When death comes, I just hope it's quick.
LAURA: Isn't it always quick?
ART: The actual death part, maybe. The stuff before can take a while.

Beat.

ART: Are you still hungry?
LAURA: Yes.

SMASH CUT TO:
EXT. DRIVE-THRU – MOMENTS LATER

They go through the drive-thru again, order more food.

SMASH CUT TO:

EXT. FAST FOOD PARKING LOT – MOMENTS LATER

They are sitting in the car, eating dessert now. Sundaes and brownies.

> **LAURA:** You think too much. Ever since I met you. Always thinking.
> **ART:** I hate thinking. Especially about death.
> **LAURA:** You always loved a good ending.
> **ART:** It's not even about closure. More...curiosity, you know? See where it all leads.
> **LAURA:** Blackness. Nothingness.
> **ART:** Oh, I don't mean the after part. That I could find out at any time. But I'm a chicken, so I'll wait until I get into a horrific accident. Or killed in a random mass shooting by some unstable asshole wanting to have his face on the news. I bet that makes you feel alive though.
> **LAURA:** Dying?
> **ART:** Yeah.
> **LAURA:** For a moment. Probably.

All right, one more scene popped into my head. This one is from the night of my thirtieth birthday:

INT. BEDROOM – NIGHT

The dog is next to Laura on the bed. Art is in the adjoining bathroom, brushing his teeth. Laura stares at the dog.

> **LAURA:** Look at him.

Art enters the frame, brushing, looking at the dog.

> **ART:** Farley. Our boy. He's so good.

LAURA: He just sits. Sits with us.
ART: He's a good boy.
LAURA: So content. You think you could ever be so content? Just to sit.
ART: All he needs is his pack. His tribe. It's ingrained in him. From his ancestors.

Art goes to spit.

LAURA: What?

Art enters the frame again.

ART: His ancestors. The wolves. He's like the wolves, sitting around the campfire.
LAURA: What are you talking about?
ART: Wolves. Sitting around a campfire. With Native Americans. Dogs evolved from wolves. You know that, right?
LAURA: They used to sit with Native Americans? Around a fire?
ART: I know I've seen depictions of it. Illustrations. Haven't you ever seen those?
LAURA: This all sounds rather idealized. You must be thinking of a movie.
ART: No, this definitely happened.
LAURA: You're thinking of *Dances with Wolves*.
ART: I've never seen *Dances with Wolves*.
LAURA: Me neither.
ART: Then what is either of us talking about?
LAURA: This is preposterous.
ART: Good word. Preposterous. I'll tell you what's preposterous—today at the diner the waitress wouldn't even melt my minestrone soup!
LAURA: Don't they have actual melts? Why must you be difficult?

Art stands there, brushing. Goes and spits.
The dog wags his tail, watching them.

Art comes back into the bedroom, turns off the light. Stands next to the bed, bends down. Kisses Laura's forehead.

LAURA: Happy birthday.
ART: Thanks, babe. Love you.
LAURA: Love you too. I'd sing you a song right now, but I'm afraid it's copyrighted.

Art smiles.

ART: I don't believe it is anymore. But we better play it safe, just in case.
LAURA: Thought that counts, anyway.
ART: I do love when you sing though.

Laura begins to sing a version of the birthday song, but with a completely different melody and lyrics.

LAURA: *Happy birthday*
You're not dead
Happy birthday
No, not yet
Congrats on being…alive
ART: Ha.
LAURA: That's all you get, birthday boy.
ART: I drank a beer in the shower today. Because of my birthday. Felt good.

Art stands up straight, scratches his belly.

ART: Gotta get some rest. Get up early. I'm thirty now.
LAURA: Early to rise.

Art turns and looks over toward the bathroom, into the mirror.
He looks at himself.
Gets in bed.

What was our big fight about? Can't say I recall.

She wanted kids. I wasn't sure yet. But that wasn't it. At least, not all of it.

For some reason, I remember a pack of gum. The act of scrounging through her handbag, looking for a pack of gum. This upset Laura, for some reason, spurring the whole thing. Perhaps she thought I was too slow, looking for the gum. Or that I never knew where gum was. Or that I was looking for gum when I was supposed to be doing something else. Whatever it was, I reacted badly. Remember spouting the phrase: "Well, Laura, I didn't know the gum represented our relationship. Wasn't aware that—in this situation—gum was a metaphor."

Anyway, the damage was likely gradual. If there even was a final argument, it was because Laura had reached her limit. She couldn't do it anymore, and I can't say I blame her. Can't imagine what it must have been like to endure my selfish bullshit, my mounting neuroses, my constant depression.

These intimate scenes I've culled from my brain, did they even happen?

We were good together. That's what I remember. There was a balance, at least in the beginning. I was her biggest fan. In turn, she made me a better person. Encouraged me to follow my passions, as she had followed hers. She wanted both of us to be happy.

Laura was the one who helped me realize I even had anxiety. That it had gotten out of control, and that I should at least consider medication, seeing a professional. These thoughts had never occurred to me before. Never comprehended I could get better, that I could feel something other than the crushing weight of the world. I thought to suffer was innate, expected. Laura showed me it didn't have to be that way.

The pills on the farm, they weren't causing me to forget. They were likely placebos. Possibly amphetamines to help keep the focus on our projects and not on what was happening around us.

If I'm being completely honest with myself—and I really am trying to be—I wanted to forget.

Does all of this explain anything? Are these flashbacks even necessary?

Suppose I can always delete them later.

Shit. Maybe the way I've written this entire novel has been a mistake.

You, the reader (hey, how are you, by the way? Hope you're doing well), doesn't need to know the thoughts and feelings of the narrator. A good story should stand on its own. Right?

Now you're going to know too much. Going to know that I'm pathetic, that I'm a phony.

Holden Caulfield would be so ashamed.

I am a phony. That much is clear, from reading this. Or am I? Me telling you all this, does it negate the phoniness? Change who I really am?

I don't know who I am anymore, who I ever was, who I was trying to be.

I am having an existential crisis, an identity crisis. A crisis crisis.

I think I'm Hemingway but I'm not concise enough. Think I'm J.D. Salinger but I'm not reclusive enough. Think I'm Camus or Kafka but I'm not existential enough. Not drunk enough to be Bukowski or stoned enough to be Burroughs. Not a romantic like Emerson or Jane Austen. Not verbose like Dickens. I'd love to be Poe or Plath, but even I'm probably not sad or moody enough for that. What about Vonnegut? Absurd, comedic, surreal. Yeah, that's closer. Sure, this book is a comedy. Look around you. Life is one big Shakespearean comedy. A tragedy. Can it be both?

Shakespeare. Now that guy could write.

Whoops, no more tangents. No time for that.

As a matter of fact, there's only one chapter left.

TWENTY

I grabbed the shotgun from the farmhand.

Our eyes locked and I watched his face go from stoic to panic.

Using the gun itself, I brought a crushing blow against the side of his head. He hit the floor and a pained wail escaped his lips, echoed through the stormy valley with the thunder.

I turned to Clorie.

"Come with me," I said.

She took my hand and with one last lingering look in each other's eyes we bolted through the open door. Beads of rain stung our faces, our clothes instantly drenched. I glanced over at Clorie. She was smiling at me. Looking at me as if seeing a new man. A man, in general. I squeezed her hand.

We were going to make it out of this place. Together.

Amazingly, the rain stopped. I gazed up at the dark storm clouds quickly departing, bright radiant sun taking their place. The entire world seemed to glow.

"Look!" Clorie shot her arm out, pointing.

There, just over the next hill: a black jeep.

Parked. Waiting, for us.

We picked up the pace, heading toward the jeep, toward freedom.

"Not so fast," we heard someone say.

Our feet skid to a halt in the dirt. Breathless, Clorie and I peered over at the impossibly tall man stepping out from behind the jeep. He was dressed dapperly in a black suit and bowler hat. The man was also holding an open umbrella over his head, beaming ear to ear with a malevolent smile. My first thought was that he resembled one of the less memorable villains from the sixties Batman TV show.

"It's not raining," I said.

"Why yes, of course," said the man in the suit, closing the umbrella and bringing it to his side. "How silly of me." He continued to grin that off-putting grin. Like Gord's grin.

This encounter was intriguing, clearly important to what was going on, plot-wise. But I was over all the bullshit, done with the quirky mysteries of the farm.

I stepped forward, clenching my fists.

"Out of our way."

"Ah, yes. You are a tenacious one, Mr. X." His voice was sugary-sweet, sickening.

"The name's Art."

"Yes, of course. And allow me to introduce myself. My name is—"

"I know who you are."

He didn't look much like Dr. Joel. Didn't have his stammer or any of his mannerisms either. He was tall though. Had to be him.

"Where's your beard?" I asked.

"Shaved it."

"Touché."

His grin widened.

"You're sick," I said.

"I believe we're forgetting who the patient is."

I clenched harder, squinting at the thin stylish silhouette in front of me. "Come on," I said. "You didn't think I knew? It's always been about me, and it's always been you behind it."

"Very good." He touched the brim of his hat, tilting it back. His eyes were Dr. Joel's eyes, all right. Peering straight through me. "But my name isn't Dr. Joel. It's Mr. Splain."

"Mister, eh?" Guess that P.H.D. on his wall was a lie too.

"There is still much to learn, Art."

"We don't care who you are," Clorie said, coming to my side. "All we want is to go home."

I smiled at her and nodded. She smiled back.

Turning my attention again to the man in the suit, I said, "That's right. We're leaving. And there's nothing you can do to stop us."

He held out his arms, gesturing around. "Have you not enjoyed your stay? Relished in the peaceful splendor of nature, the amenities of our facility? I mean—the food alone! And the *coffee*…let us not forget about the coffee."

It was good coffee. He had me there. Maybe he knew where the beans were from.

"Only the best. All for you, Art." He laughed heartily. "And look at you! Doing just fine, even without your meds. This is exactly what you needed." The smile somehow stretched even further across his face, naked and off-putting without the bushy beard. "But now, the time for harvest has come."

I winced. Was that a farm reference? Oof, this guy was a cornball.

"There must be balance, you see. Must be pain, suffering. A true artist thrives on this. On the fragility and preciousness of life, yes. But also the strife and struggle. Only then will you be able to grow and flourish." He motioned toward the crops in the distance. "A seed needs a harsh rain to fall, just as it needs the sun."

Man, he really needed to stop.

Clorie stepped forward. "Is that why you murdered Eve? For drama? Some kind of sick inspiration? Or did she find out something she wasn't supposed to?"

I stepped beside her. "Was it because she killed one of your cows?"

The man chuckled. "Such imaginations…"

Clorie shook her head in disgust. "This is all a game to you. An experiment. You're using us. Like Leonard said."

"Very good, Clorie." Mr. Splain leaned forward on his umbrella. "But for what?"

"Excuse me?"

"What am I using you for?"

Clorie and I looked at each other, shrugged.

"Oddly enough, there is some truth to Mr. Stantz's paranoid hypothesis. But there is much more than even his imagination was able to conjure. Intriguing, isn't it? In fact…I'll explain absolutely everything to you, right now. Won't take long at all, and you'll have your answers. Everything you ever wondered about the farm. Ready? Okay, so—"

"Shut it, Dr. Joel, Mr. Splain, whatever the hell you want to be called." My fists were clenched harder than ever, forearms bulging. "You're done 'splainin'. And now, we must be going."

"*Hello, I must be going…*" the strange man started to sing, waving his umbrella around like he was in a musical. Broke into a burst of giddy giggles. Clorie and I glanced over at each other again. The guy was clearly off his rocker. Really, it didn't matter what he said.

The laughter trailed off, and for the first time I saw his smile disappear.

"The bizarre deaths. The captive people. The barn warehouse. That device you saw. For fuck's sake…don't you want to know what this has all been about?"

I shrugged again. "Not really."

"…seriously?"

"Yeah, I'm good."

"Hm. Not even a little?"

"Nope."

"You can't come up with anything, can you?"

"What?"

"What?"

Mr. Splain brought a slender finger to his chin, tapping thoughtfully. "How about this," he said. "This entire farm is really one big art installation! Ha! Not a farm at all."

"Okay."

"No good?"

"Eh."

"Or. We have lured you here to milk you, harness your essence. Make Creative Juice."

Clorie furrowed her brow. "Come again?"

"Creative Juice."

"Come on now," I said. "That's not even a creative name."

Besides, no way was I going to let one of Leonard's dumb ideas become the crux of the plot.

"This is lame." I said, turning to Clorie. "Come on. Let's get outta here."

There was a twinge of desperation on Mr. Splain's face. He became momentarily unhinged, panicked.

"Art," he said. "I thought this is what you wanted. I thought you wanted...inspiration?"

"Inspire *this*!"

With this clever and dynamic catchphrase that I somehow just came up with, I lunged forward, let the dagger fly. Rather, the X-ACTO knife, the one I'd kept since cutting down the suicidal farmhand. If this were a movie, there would be a series of quick flashes now, zeroing in on the concealed X-ACTO knife with me at various points in our story. You would see my face. Waiting. Waiting for the right moment.

The moment was now.

The knife cut through the air like...well, a knife. Struck Mr. Splain/Dr. Joel directly in his jugular. His hand flew to meet the wound, no time for even a yelp of surprise. His body tensed. Blood poured, spraying all over his suit. Gasping for air, he slumped back against the jeep, slid down slowly before tipping forward into the dirt. His hat fell off, rolled toward us.

Shit. Forgot to ask about the coffee beans.

Clorie and I stared down at his lifeless body. I reared up and spit in the dirt next to him, hocking a solid loogie in the name of Eve.

The mastermind was dead. Mystery solved, as far as I was concerned. It all made sense, I was pretty sure. Probably best not to think about it too much.

Clorie was waiting for me to say something. I did.

"Well, he's dead. So that's good. Dude was crazy. Anyway. Time to go home."

Adrenaline pumping through my veins, I pulled her close, tight against my body. Dipped her back, planted a big wet one right on those waiting lips. She gazed up at me, transfixed by my rugged masculinity, my new daring demeanor. Hemingway, eat your heart out.

"Different reaction than when ol' Leonard tried to pull that on you," I joked.

"Leonard's a dick."

God, I loved her.

We climbed into the jeep. As we settled into the surprisingly comfy leather seats, thinking we were home free, the ambush happened.

A small army emerged from behind the Art Shack, dressed in black militant uniforms and armed with semi-automatic rifles. The farm's last defense, lying in wait. They moved swiftly, skillfully, firing off barrages of bullets in white-hot flashes.

I turned the key, revved the engine. Smoke billowed from the spinning back tires, which must have looked pretty cool. Then I thrust into gear and we were off. Bullets sparked and ricocheted off the jeep as we made our getaway through the open fields.

"Stick," I said.

"Huh?"

"Eve's stick."

We were about to pass Eve's gravesite. As we did, Clorie leaned out and grabbed the memorial piece of wood, placed it in my grip.

I pulled out one of my trusty cigarettes, touched it to my lips. Glanced at the militants in the rearview mirror, guns still blazing. Struck a match. Lit the cig and then the end of the stick. Respectfully. Flung it over my shoulder. Heard the *whoosh* and smiled, knowing it had made contact with my other clever little secret: the gasoline.

That's right. Your narrator Art was smarter than he let on to anyone, even you. Hell, I knew about the jeep since I saw it parked next to the barn, the night I followed the farmhand. The storyteller in me left that detail out until now, for dramatic effect.

See, after he'd gone inside I made my way over to the jeep. Pulled out the siphon I'd previously put together with spare art supplies. Drained just enough from the tank to lay a deadly trail, while still leaving enough fuel to make our escape.

It was almost too good.

The flames rose in a flash, made their way to the Art Shack. The pathetic troops were still futilely firing when the explosion happened. Poor bastards.

The heat was at our shoulders as we rode on, past crops and grazing animals, through valleys and fields, into the dense forest.

"You did it!" Clorie was laughing, crying, looking behind us.

"Did I get em, baby?"

"You sure did."

I laughed too. "Hell yeah."

Clorie was gazing over at me now, her long hair flying in the wind. "You're amazing," she said.

"Hey. I did what any other protagonist in my situation would have done. Besides, I did have some help." Wiping my eye I said softly to myself, "Thanks, Eve-Tron."

We drove on for a bit down the trail, the two of us smiling.

"Wait," said Clorie. "What blew up?"

"Huh?"

She turned to me, her smile fading. "The explosion."

"Hm?"

"I get the gasoline trail and all that…but what actually exploded?" She did that thing where she furrows her brow, thinking hard, all cute-like. "There was nothing in the shack that would make it—"

"Yeah. That explosion was pretty good, huh?"

The blast tore apart everything, the entire Art Shack decimated in an instant. It must have been beautiful; the fiery demise of our former art supplies, our original creations going up in flames as if in some sort of symbolic gesture.

Of course, all of this is an author's imagined description. I wouldn't really know.

I never looked back.

We were back home and all of a sudden it was spring.

Everything changed for me. For us.

The story I had waited my life to tell finally broke free, flowed from my fingertips like an ever-cascading fountain…similar to the fountain in the park I was once so mesmerized by. Also similar to the beautiful marble fountain we had installed in the main foyer, perfectly complimenting the classic yet contemporary bronze sculptures on either side.

It still amazes me. Somehow that aimless jobless pathetic man sitting in the park sprouted into the acclaimed and celebrated novelist you know today.

Hell, I would've been happy with a modest cult following, but the book simply caught fire (much like its explosive ending). My novel resonated with people, took on a life of its own, and your humble narrator became somewhat of an overnight sensation.

I was just glad something positive came from all the horror.

It's like Joseph Campbell once said: "A hero ventures forth from the world of common day...comes back from this mysterious adventure with the power to bestow boons on his fellow man." The classic hero's journey. Doesn't get better than that.

My boon—my gift—is my story.

After conquering the states and being transcribed into thirteen different languages, the literary critics and award-givers of the world really started to take notice. The Pulitzer was a very nice gesture, one that I graciously accepted, but I didn't write for the accolades.

All I wanted, all I've ever wanted, was to tell a story. A story that captivated, that entertained, enthralled, inspired.

Art Farm was just that.

Art Farm by Art Zazz.

Subtitle: *A Harrowing Tale of One Man's Strange, Violent—and Creative—Journey.*

Second subtitle: *The Art World will be Painted* Blood Red.

Yeah, so we capitalized on the violence angle. Clorie wasn't a big fan. At first even I debated leaving all the gory stuff in. That was before my agent reminded me that violence, much like sex, sells.

Oh, I also added a lot more sex. Like, actual sex. Not whatever it was that Clorie and I were doing. Hot, steamy stuff. Some of my best work. But that wasn't until the second printing, when I released the "Special Expanded Author's Edition."

Gotta give credit where it's due. My agent, Wes, was actually the one who suggested the title *Art Farm*. Explained that he saw the book jacket in his mind: stark, simple words, bold and blazing letters searing the front cover (like brand on cattle), illustrating the pain and brutality of the whole ordeal. All of this sounded good to me. Which is no surprise. Wes is one of the best in the biz. Makes for a mean racquetball partner too. Devastating short serve.

Anyway, I didn't really care about covers. I was just proud of the book itself. And while the thrilling climax of the novel was unanimously praised for being extremely satisfying and coherent, I was especially proud of myself for not giving in, wrapping everything up in a neat little bow. As with all the best, most enduring works, I wanted to make sure some questions remained unanswered. For certain aspects of my tale to continue to haunt readers, to linger long after the final page has been turned. This is why I never reveal if there really were scarecrows on the farm. Or the origin of the coffee beans. Were they really from Venezuela or some shit?

Of course, the farm itself is a metaphor. For what, I'll leave that up to my readers.

There was no need to let on that any of the novel was, in fact, true. Never mentioned in any of the interviews or talk shows I appeared on that it was based on actual events. Wanted the focus to be on the story. Allow the setting, characters and events to speak for themselves, let readers get lost in the world and use their imaginations. Besides, I wanted to be known as a novelist, not a memoirist.

Oh, and producer. Sold the movie rights to a big-name studio who had the whole franchise mapped out. Yes, franchise. Everything's a franchise these days. Besides, they told me they already knew the first one would be a hit, filled me in on plans for the rest of the series. It really starts to delve into the whole backstory behind the Farm Corporation in the third film, which is actually a prequel. Sure, they took some liberties with the source material, but the director seems like an enthusiastic up-and-comer, lots of energy. Reminded me of Tomas.

At first Clorie was slightly uncomfortable with our new elegant lifestyle and high position in the literary world. But she came to understand that we deserved it. I reminded her of this many, many times.

Still, this doesn't mean we've forgotten what we've been through, or those who never made it back from the farm. I make sure the gardeners maintain the stick I purchased for the veranda—a memorial to the memorial of Eve. Very high-end wood. Red Oak. Some kind of oak, anyway.

Yes, we live quite well these days in our spacious, tastefully modern loft. I really have no complaints, which is something new for me.

My anxiety is gone, panic attacks a distant memory. I have Clorie by my side and an impeccable view, looking out over the whole city.

Here, at the top of the world, our world, the walls are adorned with my awards and Clorie's paintings, not to mention awards for her paintings. Clorie was prolific before, but she's been quite the busy bee since our return to civilization. A business-investor friend once quipped rather drolly at a dinner party about their "real commercial viability."

I'm so proud of her. She is finally making it with her art. We both are.

Above all, Clorie and I are together, and that's what matters. But it's the little things, really, that still matter the most.

One sunny day, lounging by the rooftop pool, I smiled over at Clorie (her pale skin had been cute, but she looked unbelievable with a nice even tan). I said to her, "Remember the McYumYum's drive-thru when we got all that food?" My gaze drifted out over the city. "We went through twice. That was a good day."

I couldn't see her eyes through her sunglasses.

"What?" she said.

She looked so happy.

"Come on, hon." I got up, draping a towel over her shoulders. "You've got a big art show to get ready for."

My agent told me I can pull a Harper Lee, that I never have to write another book again and I'll still receive tons of accolades. Told him it was just as well, as I didn't foresee having any more ideas in the coming future.

Art Farm was it. My opus. My *raison d'être*.

My story.

Epilogue
or
A Note to Whoever Reads This

Okay. I lied.

No shit, right?

Man. Did I really quote Joseph Campbell?

I am such a blowhard.

As you may have suspected, that last chapter was bullshit.

An action-filled villain confrontation/getaway scene was my attempt at some kind of satisfying resolution. Hope you at least found it entertaining.

Fine, I'll say it. It was cheap. Like violence in general, according to Clorie.

But violence *is* real. Simply a fact of life on this brutal, disappointing speck of a planet. And it is a part of this story, whether anyone (including us on the farm) likes it or not.

Anyway, I am telling you the truth now. As much as I can.

So. Let's pick up where we left off. For serious, this time.

Promise.

I looked down at the barrel of the shotgun, then back up at the wrinkled face of the farmhand.

"Why are you killing off the different parts of my personality?" I asked.

"What?" he said.

Clorie lunged, grabbing hold of the weapon, attempting to wrestle it from his grasp. After a brief struggle he was able to wrench free, thrusting the gun upward, hitting the side of Clorie's head. She collapsed to the ground, landed on her back. The farmhand's shotgun was once again trained on me. I was already moving to Clorie, kneeling beside her motionless body. Her wide eyes stared up at me.

"Art..." she said.

Blood emerged from the gash on the side of her head, trickled down her face.

"Clorie," I said.

"I don't want to die." Her eyes were so damn big, so scared.

"Clorie..."

"..."

I kept looking down at her, trying hard to concentrate on her eyes and not the blood. I wanted to say something. Waited for my mouth to be able to move again.

"You're a really good drawer."

A smile trembled on her face.

"Thanks. You're a good writer...I think."

That was when the shotgun went off with a deafening blast and I realized her face was no longer there.

My hand went to my cheek, came away sticky and red. Blood. Clorie's blood. Jesus fucking Christ.

Guns. Violence. All the bad things. The world. We can't escape it. We never could.

My gaze drifted upwards, focusing first on the smoking barrel, then on the man.

"Come with me," he said.

The inside of the barn was bigger, brighter, and somehow even stranger than it had appeared on the night of my first glimpse through its doors. As I walked slowly down the long corridor, past rows and rows of tiny compartments bathed in an oppressive sterile glow, sounds of noisy vents and beeping machines surrounding me, I couldn't shake how oddly familiar it all seemed. *I've seen this before, done this before, felt this before.*

Really, I felt nothing. My arms were raised. My legs moved, one and then the other. Carrying my body. Moving down a white tunnel.

The heavy footsteps of the farmhand were close behind me, shotgun pointed at the small of my back.

I'm being herded, was one thought that occurred to me.

Mournful wails echoed, mixing with the industrial noises. There were people. All around me, locked inside these endless chambers. Artists.

Who are they? Are they like me? Like the others I had met and lived with?

"You killed them all," I said into the void. "Everyone I came here with."

The steady thudding of boots behind me.

"I really wanted to write a novel," I said. "Be a novelist."

Finally we reached a room at the end of the hall. The farmhand turned to the pristine metallic door, tapped a code into a mounted keypad. It slid open, revealing another chamber like the countless ones we had passed. Continuing his silent treatment, the man led me inside where my very own steadily beeping machine awaited me, next to a rather uncomfortable-looking bed.

I turned to see another two farmhands appear in the doorway. Of course they were just as silent and nondescript, their expressions just as menacingly vacant as all the others. Empty shells in matching flannel and overalls.

This is all a performance, I tried to convince myself. *An art piece.*

Well, this was it. Might as well make my futile attempt at resistance.

I'm proud to say it took all three of these spry older gentlemen to strap me down. I was a wily one, flopping around, screaming, crying, losing any remaining dignity.

Once the straps were tightened around my mid-section, legs clenched in place by steel brackets, I relaxed.

"What day is it?" I asked, for some reason.

"Tuesday," one of them said, not looking up from the restraints he was checking.

"Taco Tuesday."

This was all a bit of a blur, mind you. Though I do remember one thing vividly: once I was strapped in tight, bed adjusted so I was in an upright position, one of the farmhands suddenly reached out to me. Thought he was going to hit me so I flinched, closed my eyes. When I opened them he was standing there, holding something.

It was a pen.

All right. We are officially up to speed.

I will now write in the present tense.

So, here I am. Writing.

I know. I can't believe it either.

My hands are mostly kept free, which helps.

The farmhands, as I still call them, occasionally amble in and out of my chamber, barely glancing at each new draft. Eventually I stopped trying to engage in conversation. The most I get are grunts as they bring supplies, fiddle with knobs and various apparatuses, shove pills down my throat. Still can't tell if they're the same pills as before.

My days are spent going in and out of consciousness, awaiting each lapse into darkness as one looks forward to seeing an old friend.

Sometimes I dream.

I dream of faces, people I once knew.

Waking from a dream can be the loneliest feeling in the world.

I should write that down.

Besides the pills, I am force-fed morsels that look like dirt and taste worse.

No more buffets. No more chimichangas. No fudge sundaes or delicious coffee.

Forget about all that. Forget about the coffee beans, where they came from.

Now it is time to work, to focus.

There is nothing else.

No medication, no meditation, no masturbation.

I write until my hand is numb. Then write some more. I don't even know what I'm writing anymore.

All I know is that if I stop writing I will die. If only they'd let me.

They need me—for something. What that is I can only ponder, write about.

Still, it's nice to be needed.

Sometimes I write that what is happening to me now is my penance, a cosmic karma of some kind. Like fate, I'm not sure I believe in karma, but it doesn't matter.

How about this: I am dead already. I died when I drank that mysterious concoction in the backseat of the Oldsmobile, fell into a sleep that never ended. Or staring at that fountain in the park, I had a heart attack.

Then, of course, there's the possibility that this is all really happening.

Hard to say which scenario I prefer.

With all the pain, panic, the momentary lapses and existential dread (and the writing—we can't forget the writing), my schedule is pretty packed here at the farm. It's nice to have a routine. Though I wouldn't mind a window, a grate. A little banter with the neighbors to help blow off steam.

"Hey, what fever dream you lapse into today?"

"Same as always."

"Fuckin' A. How's your body holdin' up?"

"Ah, s'all right. Though I find the constant probing a trifle unnecessary."

"Psh. Tell me about it. They diggin' for gold?"

Hell, I'd settle for Gord as my neighbor. As long as it meant having some form of communication that wasn't between me and words on a page.

It's all very ironic, I suppose. And that's good. Irony is good. A good and respectable literary device.

The life of the Old Me I wanted so desperately to escape, it was still a life. I see that now. My own story. All I had to do was change the narrative.

Yes, hindsight is 20/20. But hindsight is all I have now.

The truth is, human beings don't have character arcs, don't change that much. Maybe they have certain realizations, gain insight or knowledge. But they'll always be the same people in the end.

I should know. I've had to face, confront, deconstruct myself many times. I've lied to myself, to you, hidden from myself, laid it all bare, said and done things I can never take back, and sometimes I've even taken them back, edited them out. All in the hope, I guess, of changing the narrative the best I can now, getting to the core of my true character, finding out who I really am.

So who am I?

I'm a self-destructive, procrastinating, egotistic, opportunistic, repugnant, indulgent, desperate, desolate, scumbag, horndog, jackass piece of shit. But I'm also a dreamer.

That's something everyone on the farm had in common. Sure, we claimed to want something real, something authentic. But what we really wanted was to live in a dream.

More irony. Good. This is good stuff.

As for narrative closure, an explanation about what the hell happened here, well…this may infuriate or confound some, but I don't know if I care. After all, isn't it the unknown that makes a story exciting? What's underneath is always more interesting than what's on the surface. The subliminal, the mythical. It's something to keep me going anyway, keep chipping away at. And who knows, the answers really might be in there somewhere.

So maybe it's a cop-out but right now this is all I have, what I'm telling you, what I've told you. Any answers I do have only lead to more questions. That's the thing about answers.

For what it's worth, this book is my attempt to write one honest sentence.

So I'll keep plugging away, cutting the fat, polishing the proverbial turd. Trying to focus on the story. The prodding helps. The probing not so much, but something else I've learned is that you can get used to anything.

Right. I should clarify. This is not the final version of this book. Oh no.

As I mentioned a long, long time ago in the introduction (that I really should delete, now that I'm thinking about it again), I am still working on it, still getting better. This epilogue was originally at least five pages longer. It's probably still too long. Shit. Again, working on it.

For now I can only hope the current draft you hold in your hands is written with some style and fervor, with integrity and honesty, that your humble author has described the events and violence that befell our group candidly and without too much embellishment.

And if not, I'll try again. What else can I do?

My story has become my nostalgia; my safe, warm blanket.

Is that also ironic? I think it might be.

This book is all I have. It is me. We are one and the same, intertwined.

This book is infinite. It will go on forever.

It's a bit like *The Neverending Story*. Only instead of luckdragons and fantastical lands, my world is full of agony and despair.

Ah, Agony. I wonder about his epic poem THE WEEPING BEAST, if anyone will ever hear it now. I like to believe he made it back to civilization, will send for help. Wanting closure is normal, natural.

I think of everyone on the farm and the ideas they had. About where ideas go when the dreamer is no longer there to dream them.

Tomas could have made a pretty interesting movie out of all of this. Even *The Grilldown* could have been, well, something.

The world will never learn of Eve-Tron and…whatever it was that she did.

And Clorie. There's a lot to remember about Clorie, but one thing she said stands out more than anything else:

"The point is not the point."

Did they have to die? As a sacrifice to the story? Because that's how the story goes?

I miss them all. Even Leonard. For the most part.

I miss McYumYum's. I miss *The Wizard of Oz* on TV. I miss my boring fuel-efficient car, the really nice garbage disposal we had at home, the stacks of novels by all the authors I admired and aspired to be.

I miss my dog, Farley. My grandmother, Gammy.

Laura.

It hurts to think her name, let alone write it. Which is probably why I avoided it for so long.

I miss her more than I ever imagined I could miss anyone or anything.

Clorie was a fascination; a romantic notion of the deep and complicated artist I thought myself to be. A would-be muse, perhaps.

Laura was...Laura.

She just was. And together we were.

Laura. Again. Laura.

The only one who loved me, tried to save me from myself. Let me know I was more than the sum of my parts, more than I gave myself credit for.

Am I rambling? I'm rambling.

I did warn you that might happen.

Anyway. Doesn't matter. Now I write for nothing, for no one.

All a bit depressing, really.

Well. At least I'm writing.

And maybe someday someone will find this book. Read it, make it all mean something.

If you are reading, well, first I want to say...thanks. Secondly, don't worry about me. This narrator will be just fine. Really, it's what I always wanted. To escape into a world of my own creation, live inside a story.

There. A happy ending...of sorts.

Okay, enough postscript. Let's rein it in. Time for my next rewrite.

Now, it may seem that my opinion did, at times, infringe on the narrative. That the description of events was somewhat biased, my thoughts a tad erratic, occasionally contradictory. However, the way I choose to see it (and isn't that all that matters?), this story is as I experienced it. Fiction or the truth, it all blends together in the end. And regardless of Leonard's opinion, I doubt a truly objective story has ever been told.

Leonard. What a putz.

Still. Suppose it's a shame he didn't get to write his version. It's possible it wouldn't have been too terrible.

Guess we'll never know, since he's dead.

I'm just dead inside. But I see that as an asset in an artist.

Besides, we're all just awful broken flesh-machines.

Hey, that's pretty good.

About the Author

Marc Dickerson is a writer and filmmaker from Philadelphia, PA. He has written short stories, graphic novels, screenplays, as well as his first prose novel, *ART FARM*. His work has appeared online and in publications such as Culture Cult Magazine and Burial Day. He lives in Bucks County, PA with his wife and daughter.

Thank you so much for reading one of our **Dark Humor** novels.

If you enjoyed our book, please check out our recommendation for your next great read!

Managed Care by Joe Barrett

Managed Care

"Witty, occasionally crass, and an unqualified delight."

-KIRKUS REVIEWS

View other Black Rose Writing titles at www.blackrosewriting.com/books and use promo code **PRINT** to receive a **20% discount** when purchasing.

BLACK ROSE writing

CPSIA information can be obtained
at www.ICGtesting.com
Printed in the USA
BVHW070114070221
599337BV00001B/84

9 781684 336722